"*Gorpp* kept my interest from the first sentence until the last…extraordinary…remarkable sense of humor..."

AGATHA CLARK, JOURNALIST FOR *NEW YORK DAILY NEWS*, REVIEWED IN AURORA ONLINE POST

"D.R. Feiler really took the time to show his love of wrestling and it shines through so clearly in this book…makes me wonder, just a bit, if the author has been a wrestler himself...I love that the dedication was to his mother because she took him to his first wrestling match…such a fun journey."

ALICIA JEANNE BOOK REVIEWS

"One of those rare books that kept me smiling almost all the way through... I say 'almost' because I was laughing my head off part of the time! Gorpp, our main character, is superbly crafted...The story is entertaining and imaginative, and the writing is solid. More Gorpp, please!"

DAWN'S BOOK REVIEWS

BY D.R. FEILER

The Grappler Chronicles

Gorpp the Grappler

Son of Blackbird

SON OF BLACKBIRD

THE GRAPPLER CHRONICLES
BOOK 2

D. R. FEILER

SOUNDS & VOICES MEDIA, LLC

Cover design by RD Custom Designs

Published by Sounds & Voices Media, LLC

eBook ISBN: 978-1-957648-03-3

Paperback ISBN: 978-1-957648-04-0

Hardback ISBN: 978-1-957648-05-7

DRFeiler.com

Dedicated to my Aunt Linda, a proud resident of Alaska and a citizen of the world.

PREFACE

LAST CHAPTER OF GORPP THE GRAPPLER

1979

"Think they're ready for wrasslin' on Enceladus?" Gabby asked Gorpp one day, as they ate lunch by the pool at the Don Cesar.

"It's a very different place," he said.

"Maybe we could bring a group of wrestlers from Earth and take them on a tour of the rings of Saturn. It probably wouldn't be much stranger for a lot of them than going to Japan."

Sometimes, he couldn't tell if she was teasing him. It wouldn't be unusual. But, sometimes she both meant what she was saying and was teasing him at the same time. Humans, it turned out, were more complex than the original reconnaissance indicated. He was pretty deadpan himself. They made a good couple.

She put her fork down, even though the crab cakes were delicious. She reached out and held his hand in hers. "Maybe it's time for a new challenge. We became the champions of my world. Maybe it's time to test our mettle on yours. Overalls could be our Steve Levey."

He looked at her intently and she could feel his pulse in her hand.

"I want to see the geysers of Enceladus. I want to go to your caverns under the sea. I want to see where you were born. Where you grew up. What parks you played at. Where you graduated high school. I wanna meet your folks."

Again. Teasing him with all of her Earth references. But meaning every word just the same. He squeezed her hand and was reminded again of how grateful he was to have her as his wife.

"Are you going to answer me?"

He took his hand away, picked up his fork and took a bite of Eggs Benedict, looked out at the surf and breathed in the salt air from the Gulf. "There's only one way to make it work," he said.

Gabby smiled and said, "kayfabe."

CHAPTER 1

APRIL 23, 1982

GORPP LANDED his small vessel just off Duval Street in Key West, and opened the airlock. He and Gabby stepped out to a spring breeze carrying the scent of salt air and the sounds of a crowd celebrating. They walked onto the main drag and saw hundreds of people cheering for a plain looking man with glasses, a small flag in his shirt pocket and a microphone, speaking in impassioned tones in front of the Greater Key West Chamber of Commerce.

"I proclaim that Key West shall now be known as the Conch Republic," he said.

"What's going on?" Gabby said.

Gorpp didn't respond. They mingled with the crowd and the sound from the public address system carried the man's voice to them with more volume.

"We secede from the United States. We've raised our flag, given notice, and named our new government—"

"Seriously," she said. "What is going on?"

Gorpp looked at her but still didn't respond.

"We're not a fearful people. We're not a group to cringe and whimper when Washington cracks the whip with contempt and unconcern. We're Conchs, and we've had enough!" He was really picking up a head of steam now and the crowd ate it up. Gabby noticed one person sporting a shirt that said, **WE SECEDED WHERE OTHERS FAILED**.

"Big trouble has started in much smaller places than this," the man said.

"That is true," Gorpp said to Gabby.

Gabby didn't respond. She turned to a man next to her with a shaggy beard, Hawaiian shirt, captain's hat and cigar. "What's going on here?"

"Haven't you heard?" he said. "We're seceding from the union!"

"Who is?" she said.

"Key West. From now on, we're going to be known as the Conch Republic. Mayor, I mean, Prime Minister Wardlow," he pointed to the man with the microphone, "he's standing up to The Gipper." He snorted. "Wardlow's the only politician I ever saw worth a damn. I'm glad I voted for him. How often do you get to say that?"

"I am calling on all my fellow citizens here in the Conch Republic to stand together, lest we fall apart, fall from fear, from a lack of courage, intimidation by an uncaring government whose actions show it has grown too big to care for people on a small island."

The crowd erupted. Gabby turned back to the man beside her.

"What's this all about?" she asked, still looking around, trying to make sense of a tourist town in Florida, where everyone from Ernest Hemingway to Harry Truman had taken up residence over the years, seceding from the union.

"Damn checkpoint," he said, pointing, as if she would be able to see it. "Up on US Route 1 in Florida City, you know, right there in front of Skeeter's Last Chance Saloon. They're gonna treat us like we ain't natural citizens, well then, Mayor, damnit, I mean Prime Minister Wardlow, he's sending a message to Ronnie, the Border Patrol and all them bureaucrats up in Washington, they can all go to hell. We'll be just fine on our own if that's how they're gonna treat us."

Gabby looked around again, trying to make sense of it. The energy in the crowd felt more like Mardi Gras than a revolution. People wore silly hats or swim trunks. They drank beer and Margaritas.

"What's the roadblock for? What are they looking for?"

"Some say drugs, cause it makes a good talking point for Nancy and her 'Just Say No' campaign, but what it's really about—" He stopped himself and took a good look at Gorpp for the first time, then resumed in a hushed voice, "is illegal aliens."

Gorpp and Gabby shared a look.

"Hey, wait a second," the man said. He inhaled on his cigar and pointed at Gorpp. "You're that alien wrestler guy, aren't you?"

"Yes," Gorpp said.

The man let out an I'll be damned, burst of laughter. The Prime Minister had finished his speech and a mix of reggae from a nearby bar and mariachi music from a band of street musicians mingled in the air with whoops and hollers of inebriated revelry.

The man with the beard and cigar regarded Gorpp again thoughtfully.

"You best not try to go up through that checkpoint, if you take my meaning. I mean, no offense but..." He trailed off and shrugged at Gorpp.

Gorpp didn't respond.

The crowd was starting to move around them, like a living thing. Some headed for Sloppy Joe's, a favorite haunt of Hemingway's. Some danced in the streets in drag, and some were doing media interviews with the likes of Michael Putney and even Mort Castle. The New York anchorman had jumped on an Eastern Airlines flight as soon as the rumblings of secession started. Eastern was the only airline with service to the island. Castle liked being the first national correspondent on the scene when history was unfolding, so he kept track of these kinds of things.

The man beside them brushed long and oily hair out of his eyes to reveal wraparound sunglasses.

"Don't worry," he said. He looked around at the band of hippies, drag queens, artists and misfits who made up the newly formed Conch Republic. He put an earnest hand on Gorpp's shoulder. "You're gonna fit right in around here."

Gorpp didn't respond. He squeezed Gabby's hand as if to say, let's move along.

Their new friend sensed his restlessness and added, "Oh wait, citizen, before you go, you want one of these cigars?" He reached into the pocket of his Hawaiian shirt. "Made right here on the island. Better then Cubans." He tucked the hand-rolled cigar into Gorpp's hand.

To Gabby's surprise, Gorpp inspected it, nimbly removed the cap with his knife-like fingernails and placed it in his mouth.

"Got a light?" he asked the man.

With a familiar motion, the man produced a butane lighter from his shirt pocket and lit Gorpp's cigar.

Gabby looked at him.

"I'm celebrating," he said.

"Long live the Conch Republic!" the man shouted, eliciting a few cheers from those in earshot. Then he turned back to the couple. "Comrades, I bid you adieu. I've got a date with a blender, some rum and a balcony with a great view of the Gulf. Come to think of it, you're welcome to join me if you'd like."

"We'd love to," Gabby said. "But we've got a date of our own, with an old friend."

"May the road rise with you," he said with a flourish of his cigar, tossing his long hair out of his eyes again. He started to turn away, then said, "They call me 'Duck,' by the way. Bunch of quacks if you ask me!"

Gorpp had never displayed an appreciation for wordplay or subscribed to the human social convention of feigning an insincere response out of a sense of obligation to be courteous. Gabby offered an obligatory chuckle. Gorpp tugged on her hand again, this time more forcefully. Gabby tugged right back.

"Say, Duck," can you spare another one of those?"

"You betcha!" Duck produced another cigar for the lady but she waved off the light.

"It's for a friend," she said.

CHAPTER 2

GORPP AND GABBY STROLLED, hand in hand, up Duval Street. Gorpp smoking his cigar and eliciting the occasional jubilant response from a fan or at least someone who recognized him as some kind of celebrity. Only the real wrestling fans knew Gabby was also known as 'Firefly,' a women's champion and promoter in her own right.

They passed a juggler with a snake draped over his shoulders and a vendor selling Conch Republic passports from a converted hotdog stand before making their way up a quiet side street with little bungalows on stilts by the water. They slowed as they approached a hacienda-style bungalow with Spanish tiles on the roof. It was small but in a beautiful spot. They walked up and rapped on the door.

"Hold on!" they heard the old man grumble as he stomped to the door, but when he opened it and saw Gorpp and Gabby, those hardened features gave way to a grin. "Well, I'll be damned," Ernie said. "If it isn't the long lost vagabonds of the wrestling world. Come on in to my retirement home." When Ernie sold to Gabby, he retired from decades in the wrestling business, and moved from Tampa to Key West.

Ernie sat at his wooden banker's swivel desk chair and

Gorpp and Gabby sat in two folding metal chairs that had been leaning up against the wall.

"You kids picked a hell of a day to visit," Ernie said. "You know what happened today, what's going on?"

"We saw the Mayor's speech," Gabby said. "And one of the locals filled us in on the rest."

"This stunt's gonna more than make up for any tourism dollars they lost to the roadblock. This Mayor's brilliant if you ask me. Kind of mind we need more of in our business these days," he said wistfully, then reached for his pack of Salems.

"Hey, I brought you something," Gabby said and handed him Duck's cigar.

Ernie took a close look at it. "This is a good cigar. Where'd you get this?"

"A friend," she said.

Ernie prepped it, lit it, inhaled, and then blew the smoke out the open window to float away over the Gulf. He looked out the window for a few moments, then back to his visitors.

"So, what brings you calling on an old man in the Conch Republic?"

"We want to take wrestling to Enceladus," Gabby said, very matter of fact. "We need your advice about how to do it. Who to bring? What to bring. All of it. We need one of our late night brainstorming sessions like we used to have with Bobby at the Cuban place in Ybor City."

Ernie just looked at them, first at her, then at Gorpp, then back to Gabby. They'd talked about how he would react. They'd wouldn't have been surprised if he told them it was a ludicrous idea, or that he was retired and didn't want to think about wrestling anymore, but for some reason, they hadn't anticipated what he did say.

Ernie looked out the window, took another puff on the cigar, exhaled, then tapped the ashes in his ashtray already full of cigarette butts. He looked long and hard at Gorpp before he spoke.

"So, you're serious? You really are an out of this world alien?"

"Yes," Gorpp said.

Ernie looked down at the floor, then set the cigar down in the ashtray and let it smolder. His knees creaked and cracked, from old ring injuries, as he stood up. He paced the few steps toward the window and let the salt air push his whisps of white hair back. He kept looking out at the ocean as he spoke.

"All those years, when you were wrestling," he said. "I never really thought about it, I guess. Never allowed myself to think about it. I just thought it was the greatest gimmick ever and the money kept rolling in. Calvin and the other owners got to be a pain in the ass after a while but it seemed like no matter what we did you just got more popular. That's all I could think about. Or all I did think about anyway."

He turned to face them.

"It wasn't until I retired and came here and had all this time, this solitude and quiet, except for the waves and the occasional parade on Duval Street, that I really started questioning it. I got to where I couldn't believe you were and I couldn't believe you weren't. Sometimes my own head don't make any sense to me."

Ernie put his hands on his knees and leaned down, staring right into Gorpp's big almond eyes.

"Son of a bitch," he said, then slapped his knees as he slowly straightened up. "So, all this time, you're really a bonafide in the flesh Martian?"

"I'm from the moon of Enceladus, in the rings of Saturn," Gorpp said.

"Right, right. But you really are? That's what you're telling me." He looked at Gabby. "You knew?" he said.

"Yes," she said.

"You're married to an alien?"

She looked at Gorpp and then back to Ernie. "Yes," she

said with a quiet conviction and a smile curving the corners of her mouth.

Ernie had a kind of wild look in his eyes, like a storm was brewing in his corneas. "How you get along with the in-laws there, Gorpp?" he said. "You two lovebirds go home for the holidays? Say grace at the Millers' dining room table? Help trim the tree?, do you?"

"Honestly, my parents have been tremendously understanding. We didn't realize you didn't know, I mean, you've known all this time," she said.

"I guess I have," he said. "I just never allowed myself to really believe it. And to think about all the things that would have come with that, you know?"

Outside they heard fireworks and hollers in the distance. Ernie seemed to snap out of it.

"Listen, let's go get some shrimp and Conch Fritters, drink some beer and smoke cigars with the locals and we can talk about all of this. It's just good to see you both. I'm glad you're here. What do you say?"

CHAPTER 3

WHAT STARTED as dinner and beers at a little joint off Duval called the Mermaid's Tail lasted into the wee hours. By the time Gorpp and Gabby helped Ernie back to his retirement cottage by the sea, and into bed, the three had mapped out a plan to take Heavyweight Championship Wrestling to Saturn's sixth largest moon, Gorpp's home world of Enceladus.

A lot had changed in the world of professional wrestling between 1979 and 1982. The Unified Syndicate of Professional Wrestling that started out as a Northeast territory was fast on its way to becoming a monopoly, buying up or otherwise pushing out one regional territory after another. A lot of wrestlers who'd had secure positions in their respective territories were being forced out, moved down the food chain or leaving professional wrestling because they no longer recognized what it was becoming.

Gorpp and Gabby hadn't seen Bobby since he served as the officiant at their wedding at the Don Cesar. Bobby had been Ernie Cantrell's righthand man, his enforcer and his most trusted confidante and coconspirator. His in-ring career had been cut short years before by an injury but he was still one tough son-of-a-gun and nobody knew the business better, inside or outside the ring. Most observers had assumed, when Cantrell finally retired, Bobby would take over Heavyweight Championship Wrestling from Florida. No one guessed it would be Gabby Miller, the Firefly. And once that news got out, most in the wrestling business assumed Bobby would feel slighted, but he didn't. He'd recommended her.

The sun was coming up over the water, a melted pink orb, when they got Ernie tucked into his bed. Gabby went ahead and put a pot of coffee on for him and left a note on the counter.

Thank you for the hospitality, the advice and the war stories. It's good to see retirement is agreeing with you. – Love G&G

As they were getting ready to leave, Gabby noticed a pile of typing paper on a small desk by the window next to an IBM Selectric typewriter. The top page had these words centered at the top:

My Life In and Out of the Ring
by Ernie Cantrell

"Did you see this?" Gabby asked Gorpp.

"Yes," he said.

There was a stack of pages underneath. She wondered if he'd finished it. It was tempting to turn the page but she would never have invaded his privacy that way. They left the bungalow and met just a few revelers who had stayed up through the night as they walked back to Gorpp's vessel. There was a hippie-looking guy with a Grateful Dead shirt and white dreadlocks staring at Gorpp's ship and them as they approached. They boarded and before the hatch sealed they heard him utter, "Far out!" Then they lifted off and flew over the traffic still backed up at the Florida City roadblock.

"Good thing we didn't drive," Gabby said, then she laughed. "You know, illegal alien."

In no time, they were making their descent onto the roof of the Ambassador Hotel in Tampa, where Gorpp had first landed when he'd gone AWOL from the occupation and decided to become the champion of Earth. They entered the building from a door on the roof and took the elevator to the lobby. Here, so close to the Bayfront Armory, plenty of people recognized them both, but they didn't get hassled too much between the lobby and the front drive where the bellman hailed them a cab.

"Harbour Island Marina" Gabby told the driver.

CHAPTER 4

WHEN THEY ARRIVED, Gorpp gave the cabbie and exorbitant tip, as he usually did since he saw no value in money himself but recognized how much humans coveted it. They walked out on the docks. Ernie didn't know what slip number Bobby had but he knew the name he gave the boat he'd bought to go into the charter fishing business. *The Mildred Burke.* Burke had been arguably the greatest female wrestler of all time, at least until Firefly came along.

The serenity of pelicans and seagulls gliding over the calm water was broken by a shout. "We want our money back, asshole!" They looked up just a few slips ahead and saw someone on a boat yelling and pointing his finger at a man with sandy blonde hair and an expression of stern resolve. "If you don't give us our goddamn money back I might just have to give you another scar on the other side of your face to match that ugly one you've already got." They'd found *The Mildred Burke*, and Bobby.

The guy yelling at him had a few buddies with him, holding fishing gear. Bobby appeared nonplussed by his unhappy customer's outburst or his threat as he secured *The Mildred Burke* to the dock.

"Hey, asshole. You hear me talking to you?"

Bobby finished what he was doing, then stood up and faced the guy.

"You gentlemen are getting off my boat now. If you want to do it without getting wet I wouldn't hesitate."

"We're not leaving without our money, asshole."

Bobby took a step toward the guy and easily ducked a roundhouse punch it looked like he'd thrown in slow motion. The force of the missed blow caused him to stagger forward and Bobby gave him a swift kick in the ass that sent him tumbling over the railing and into the water. After that, he used his foot to swipe the guy's rod and tackle into the drink behind him, then turned to face his friends. It was still morning but they were clearly drunk. The first guy was splashing around in the water, spitting expletives and threats and dirty salt water. There were three still onboard, but not for long.

It almost looked to Gabby like a *Three Stooges* routine, the way Bobby made these guys look so foolish in such short order. Without hurting any of them he had them all off his boat and in the water in a matter of a few seconds. He followed that by picking up the remaining rods and tackle and tossing those overboard as well. He hadn't even broken a sweat. Then, as if he'd been aware of them the whole time, he casually turned to Gorpp and Gabby.

"Hey, strangers." He motioned to the gangplank. "Welcome aboard."

As the couple stepped aboard, Bobby unmoored the rope he'd just fastened to the dock and headed for the helm. "Let's get away from all this racket," he said and soon the flailing, splashing and yelling were far behind them. Bobby navigated the channel past Marjorie Park Marina and Davis Islands into Hillsborough Bay.

With the marina out of sight and nothing but the ocean breeze and the glint of the sun on the calm bay waters around them, Bobby dropped anchor and invited them to sit down with him at a simple table bolted to the deck.

"So," he said, "what brings you two back to town?"

"We want to take wrestling to Gorpp's home world. We're looking to put together a stable of talent both in and out of the ring. We went to talk to Ernie about it yesterday and we all agreed you needed to be our first stop."

"I thought you said Ernie was your first stop."

"For counsel," Gabby said. "To make sure we were thinking about how to approach this the right way. You're our first stop because you're the most important person for us to recruit onto this tour."

"You kids come up with an angle yet?"

"With Ernie," Gabby said. "The takeover of Saturn and it's moons and colonies. They will have heard of the occupation and planned takeover of Earth. We'll sell this as a counterstrike on their soil. It'll be irresistible."

"Wait. Hold on a second. What occupation and planned takeover of Earth?"

Gorpp and Gabby just looked at each other.

"That wasn't just an angle?"

"It's nothing you need to worry about," Gabby said.

Bobby didn't look convinced but he didn't pursue it further.

"Ok, sure. I won't worry about it. So, you went to see Ernie yesterday? At his place in Key West? Were you two part of the revolution, or whatever, down there?"

"We were there for the Prime Minister's proclamation," Gabby said. "But no, we didn't know anything about it until we landed."

"In your spaceship? Or should I say, the family car?"

"In my vessel, yes," Gorpp replied.

"And you're planning to take it and a bunch of wrestlers to, where is it?"

"The where is Enceladus, the sixth-largest moon of Saturn.

But my vessel is only large enough for two. We'll need something much bigger," Gorpp said.

"I don't think Hertz rents spaceships," Bobby said.

"I have a plan to acquire an adequate means of transport," Gorpp said.

"Do tell."

"My people have an armada of vessels, large and small, both under what you call the Bermuda Triangle in the Atlantic Ocean, and above your atmosphere. Theft is unknown in our culture. So, I plan to simply take a ship that will suit our needs. They won't know what to make of it until we have enough of a head start that it shouldn't matter."

"I'm just going to play this out," Bobby said. "Why do your people have such a presence here?"

"It's an occupation."

"But I shouldn't be concerned."

"No," Gorpp said. "They won't make their presence widely known in your lifetime."

"Good thing I don't have kids, I guess."

Gorpp didn't respond.

"Alrighty, then, now that we've covered that, let me wrap my mind around this. You want to put a tour together, like we would if we were going to Japan, but you're going half way across the galaxy?"

"No, just halfway across your solar system," Gorpp said. "Halfway across the galaxy wouldn't be practical."

"Oh, sure. Of course. What was I thinking?"

Gabby looked at Gorpp. "It was a rhetorical question. You don't need to answer it."

"I have to ask," Bobby said. "What did the old man make of all this?"

"Well," Gabby said, "he was pretty taken aback. Somehow he'd never really allowed himself to come to terms with the fact that Gorpp isn't from Earth."

"That sounds right," Bobby said. "He stayed pretty

focused on his cigarettes, his safe and making sure we were putting asses in the stands."

"Can I ask you something, Bobby?" Gabby said.

"Sure."

"You know Ernie as well as anybody. Probably better than his son."

"I did."

"Do you think we should have invited him?"

"He's retired."

"From wrestling, yes. But I mean, do you think we should have invited him for the chance to visit another world?"

"From what you've told me it sounds like he was having enough trouble just accepting the fact that Gorpp here wasn't really from Toledo or even Transylvania. I don't know that that old curmudgeon would have adapted well to all of that."

Gorpp looked at Bobby intently.

"What is it?" Gabby asked him.

"He's right," Gorpp said.

"Why do you say that?"

Instead of answering Gabby, Gorpp turned to Bobby. "Will you join us?"

Bobby looked out at the water, then got up and walked over to the railing, still with his back to them. When he spoke he didn't turn back around.

"Ernie was always fair with me," he said. "When he sold you the territory, I had enough saved to take my time deciding what came next. Our business, at least on this planet, has become unrecognizable to me. The Syndicate is dismantling the territories one by one. I guess I don't have to tell you. Anyway, I needed a change." He tapped his hand on the railing a couple times. "So I bought this boat. I know my way around boats from my time in the service. Hell, I grew up on this bay, and I thought it would be a nice way to keep some money coming in and get to spend my days out on the water."

"How's it working out?" Gabby said.

Bobby laughed. "They're not all as bad as that bunch of ambulance chasers you saw back at the marina but I can't say it's what I thought it would be. Most of my customers don't know a marlin from a Martian, no offense," he said with a quick glance at Gorpp.

Gorpp didn't respond.

"And most of 'em start drinking at sunrise when we set out, like that bunch did. They can be pretty obnoxious when the fish aren't biting. And when they are, I spend my day sliding around in more blood and guts than I'd care to. It's not all sunsets and Rum Runners, you know?"

"So you'll come?" Gabby said.

"Now hold on, I didn't say that. Let me think about it. You two see how the rest of the recruiting goes and let me know when you've, shall we say acquired, your spaceship. I'll tell you then."

CHAPTER 5

WHEN THEY GOT BACK to the marina there was no sign of the lawyers Bobby had tossed overboard. Gorpp and Gabby helped him get things in order on *The Mildred Burke,* then he gave them a lift to Ybor City, to the Columbia Restaurant. It was late afternoon and Bobby assured them Steve Levey could be found there almost every day. Number two on the list. They thanked Bobby and made their way inside. Sure enough, there was Levey, a cigar in one hand and martini in the other, holding court at the historic restaurant's ornate bar, and wearing his trademark floral print silk shirt and burgundy sport coat.

One of the patrons listening to Levey's tales pointed when Gorpp and Gabby approached, and then heads started turning. At first Levey looked annoyed, but once he saw who it was, he gave the first couple of professional wrestling a royal welcome. Like flipping a switch, he was back at the Bayfront calling an historic contest and imparting to the crowd a reverence for what they were witnessing that left them knowing in their gut they'd been a part of something special.

"Ladies and gentlemen, what an honor and a privilege to be able to welcome two of the great world champions in the history of professional wrestling, Gorpp the Grappler and Firefly!"

The barflies, hangers on, waitstaff and diners in earshot all played their part and applauded, heralding the arrival of still the biggest draws in wrestling, despite having been inactive as the Syndicate gobbled up more and more territories, but not the services of Gorpp or Gabby.

"Thank you," Gabby said, making eye contact with a few people in the crowd. She raised the hand Gorpp was holding like a presidential candidate does with his running mate when they get the nomination at the convention. Once they made their way to Levey, the patrons at Columbia Restaurant respected their privacy and Gorpp and Gabby were able to exchange greetings with Levey without feeling they were being eavesdropped on. Despite that, when Gabby explained they were there to talk about a unique business proposition, Levey quickly made arrangements to move them into the Don Quixote Room, where he had had many confidential business meetings over the years. You'd have thought he owned the place.

Once they were settled into a private room, Levey had a round of the Columbia's famous Nineteen-o-fives served to each of them. He explained they were martinis, with Tito's Handmade Vodka, and the olives marinated and stuffed with Cabrales cheese. Levey offered Gorpp a cigar and he accepted. The two took their time observing the customs of properly preparing the cigar before smoking it. Once they'd settled in, Levey took a sip of his drink, set it aside, put his elbows on the table and leaned in over the small candle in the center of the table.

"I know you two aren't the types for a casual visit. Let's get down to business," Levey said.

This time, Gorpp teed things up.

"As a native of Saturn's moon, Enceladus, I came to Earth and took over, reigned as the Heavyweight Champion of the World. Books will be written about it. Now, Earth is ready for a counterstrike. We will take a roster of Earth's best wrestlers on a tour of Enceladus itself, and one of them will vow to take over there as I did on Earth. Nothing could be more alien to my people and their curiosity will demand their attention. We'll put asses in the stands, so to speak, like you've never seen, Mr. Levey."

Announcer extraordinaire Steve Levey was seldom left speechless but this was more than he'd ever heard Gorpp say in years of calling his matches.

"Mr. Levey," Gabby picked up the thread. "We've been to see Ernie and we talked about how important your voice, your imprimatur, your credibility will be to make this venture a success."

"I've always dreamed of going to the stars," Levey said. "I live a life where I don't have much need of feeling jealous but when Neil Armstrong stepped foot on the moon, I wished it could have been me. If you're telling me there's a ship taking off for the stars, to visit a new world, you won't be able to keep me away. I can be ready tonight."

Gabby reached out and squeezed Levey's hands. "Thank you!" she said. "This means so much to us."

"It's the opportunity of a lifetime and I will be forever grateful to you both for including me," Levey said.

They joined him back in the main dining room where he insisted on buying them several more rounds of Nineteen-o-fives and then ordered them all a buffet-style dinner with Nineteen-o-five salads with extra Worcestershire and garlic dressing, Cuban Black Bean Soup, Mahi Mahi Cubanas and then flan, key lime pie and strong Cuban coffee for dessert. He kept them there until almost midnight, watching flamenco dancers in a celebration to rival the secession of the Konch Republic. "To the stars!" was Levey's oft repeated toast that night. At one point, in the candlelight, it looked to her like Levey had tears in his eyes.

CHAPTER 6

NEXT, they were headed south again, this time to Miami to see John White Eagle, a legend in Miami and in the world of Heavyweight Championship Wrestling. He first got noticed by Ernie Cantrell, on the independent circuit, wrestling alligators in the Everglades. And he could lay claim to the first really meaningful match of Gorpp's career. They had had more than one clash that would be long remembered. Gabby eventually sold the Florida territory to him to consolidate with his Southeast territory that was active in neighboring states, Alabama and Louisiana for the most part. But even with such a storied stronghold for wrestling, from Miami to Montgomery as he liked to say, he couldn't stop the unstoppable force of the Syndicate. First he sold to them. Now he worked for them. And time marched on.

When Gorpp and Gabby arrived in Miami and started asking around for White Eagle, they quickly learned he was in New York. Now that he worked as a road agent for the USPW, he was seldom home in his native South Florida. The trip from Miami to New York, with the technology in Gorpp's vessel, took only moments longer than it took to program the destination into the ship's computer.

As they landed in Central Park, the brilliant greens and pinks of the leaves came into clear view. Spring had arrived in the Big Apple. When they opened the airlock in a thick grove of trees, a chilly wind swept into the cabin though it was a clear sunny day in the home of USPW headquarters. They found White Eagle in warehouse a few blocks from Madison Square Garden where the Syndicate did a lot of their pre-taped matches and promos. A low-end sound studio. A few people on the crew pointed and smiled, as if to say to the person standing next to them, *can you believe who just walked onto our set?*

Gabby hardly recognized John with a big trench coat and black boots on. This Seminole Indian who grew up in Florida swampland even had a scarf wrapped around his neck. You'd have thought it was twenty below in there though it was closer to fifty degrees. He was in an intense discussion with one of the younger wrestlers. When he looked up and saw them, he broke off immediately. "I'll be right back," he told the up and comer.

"I can't believe it," he said, walking toward them with his arms spread for a big group hug. Gabby hugged him back with a big smile. Gorpp tolerated the embrace.

"How are you doing up north here?" Gabby asked.

"I'm freezing my Florida balls off!" White Eagle said. "At this point, I'd kiss a Cottonmouth on the lips just for a little warmth in my bones." He looked around the room as if his coworkers were all inmates in an asylum.

Gabby leaned in close, making it look like another warm embrace from an old friend, knowing staff, talent, management and probably the lighting guy were watching them, trying to hear this conversation.

"We're here to talk to you about a tour we're putting together. It's big," Gabby whispered. Then she leaned back out to a comfortable distance.

"I gotta get back to work." He pointed back to the wrestler

who stood waiting for him. "Why don't you come by my hotel later? There's a nice big fireplace in the lobby. We can meet there, catch up." White Eagle pulled a pen out of his pocket and jotted down the name of the hotel and the address on the back of a very official-looking USPW business card.

"We look forward to it," Gabby said.

Gorpp and Gabby walked all over the city, hand in hand, talking, sightseeing, and even signing a few autographs. White Eagle said he wouldn't be available until about eight o'clock so they had plenty of time to explore. They went to the top of the Empire State Building, saw the bright lights on Broadway and the Statue of Liberty across Hudson Bay. For dinner, they had a slice of New York pizza, then they headed for the hotel to meet White Eagle.

They found him, arms spread out across a big leather couch in front of a crackling fire. The lobby bustled with activity and the three were able to settle in without garnering too much notice. When White Eagle stood to greet them he peeled off the wool scarf and big trench coat and tossed them onto the back of the couch. Gorpp and Gabby, plenty warm from their day of walking the city, sat down beside him.

"So," he said. "Tell me what brings you to see me all the way up here in New York City."

"We're going to take wrestling to Gorpp's home world. We're putting together our crew and we want you with us," Gabby said.

"You're taking wrestling to space?"

"To Enceladus," Gorpp said.

"Ha! I love it!" White Eagle slapped Gorpp's knee. "You two are the best in the business. The best. What an angle. Have you tipped off Howie? He's gonna want to come, you know?"

"He's on our list," Gabby said. "First, we want to get everything, everyone in place. You ready for a break from the USPW?"

"How long a break we talking about?"

"The trip will take a few Earth weeks," Gorpp said. "The duration of the tour will depend on our reception. Then a few weeks to return. I would estimate about three of your months."

"It's not every day I get offered a job on another planet."

"Enceladus is a moon," Gorpp said.

"Your boyfriend doesn't have much sense of humor. You ever notice that?" White Eagle said to Gabby.

"Husband," she said. "My husband doesn't have much sense of humor. And yes, I've noticed."

"This is a serious offer?"

"Yes," she said. "We've been thinking about it for quite a while now. And we're ready to give it a go."

"We've conquered Earth," Gorpp said. "It's time for new frontiers."

"Would you want me in the ring or as a road agent?"

"We want you there to help us make sure it's a success," Gabby said. "Once we know who we have we'll make the decisions about how best to utilize talent. You'll help us figure it all out."

"Who do you have so far?"

"We've just started to put the team together but I can tell you Steve Levey will be calling the matches."

"He's the best."

"No doubt about it," she agreed.

"What about Bobby?"

"We'll get him."

"I'm in," White Eagle said. He rubbed his hands together in front of the fire. "As long as it's warm there, I'm in."

CHAPTER 7

Gorpp and Gabby walked through the streets of the city after dark, still hand in hand. They passed some shady looking characters but Gabby felt safe with Gorpp. The next morning, in their hotel, Gabby awoke with a question on her lips.

"Didn't you once tell me it was three hundred fifty degrees below zero on Enceladus?"

"Yes," he said. "On the surface."

"Let's not mention that to White Eagle before we leave," she said.

Gorpp looked at her. He didn't smile, per se, but she had come to recognize a certain glint in his almond-shaped eyes. "Kayfabe," he said. *Keep the secret.*

As long as they were in New York, there were a couple of other people they wanted to see. The first was Howie Shows, the dean of wrestling journalism. Only a few old timers, like Ernie Cantrell, could even remember a time before Howie Shows' *World Wrestling Digest*. The next morning, they found Howie with his crazy white tufts of hair and pencil behind his ear, buried under a mountain of back issues of the *Digest*, typing away on an IBM Selectric typewriter that looked a lot like Ernie's but with a lot more miles on it.

"Stop the presses!" Howie shouted when the two squeezed their way into his cramped office. "To what do I owe the pleasure of this visit to *World Wrestling Digest* headquarters? Wait! Before you answer that, you have to take a picture with me for my wall." He pointed to a crooked row of cheap eight-by-ten frames with prints of him with the legends of the squared circle, from Black Jack Tolliver to John White Eagle to Robert "Bear Claw" Monroe. Howie got the building super to take their picture with his Canon he used at ringside.

"Now, what can I do for the first family of professional wrestling?"

Howie was tucked back behind his desk and Gorpp and Gabby sat in chairs opposite him with stacks of magazines, promotional photos and other assorted paraphernalia teetering all around them.

"Mr. Shows, what would you say if I told you we were taking professional wrestling to another world, far from Earth?"

"I would say how do I get a seat on that rocket ship?"

It was as simple as that. He never doubted the veracity of their invitation or had a second thought about accepting it. He seemed almost as excited as Steve Levey. They shook hands in that cramped office and promised to be in touch. Howie was on board.

They asked Howie for a suggestion for lunch and he told them he knew just the place. He took them to Russ & Daughters, the premiere Jewish deli in a city full of connoisseurs for nearly seventy years. And it was the first business in the country to have "and daughters" instead of "and sons" in the name. Howie said he thought it would be a fitting destination for the first woman owner of a territory in Heavyweight Championship Wrestling's history, especially since her father, the good Dr. Miller, had himself been an investor when she bought the Florida territory form Ernie

Cantrell. But none of that would have mattered if Russ & Daughters hadn't had the best belly lox and babka in the city.

Their next stop was the matches at Madison Square Garden that night. They'd heard a lot of buzz about the USPW's new sensation, the masked terror, Machete Marquez. He had a chiseled physique, a short fuse and a tomahawk chop that could rival Wahoo McDaniel's. They wanted to see him up close before they decided if they'd try to poach him from the Syndicate.

Standing in the back, trying not to be noticed, Gorpp and Gabby both wore hooded jackets and stayed in the shadows. Standing in the back like this reminded Gorpp of the first matches he saw at Bayfront Armory. When Machete Marquez burst through the curtain and started bounding to the ring it felt like an electric charge igniting the crowd.

"Well, the ladies are impressed," Gabby said. She could hear the catcalls from all over the Garden as Marquez gracefully hopped over the top rope into the ring.

"Are you impressed?" Gorpp asked.

"Jealous much?" Gabby teased.

He didn't respond.

"Ernie would say he puts asses in the stands," Gabby said.

Gorpp surveyed the Garden and couldn't find an empty seat anywhere.

Marquez was graceful, vicious and truly electrifying. He dispatched of his opponent easily. After the matches they found him holding court at the Plaza Hotel bar. He had women and men fawning over him. He wore a designer suit with an open collar, gold chain and, of course, his mask. *Kayfabe.*

"A word, Mr. Marquez?" Gabby's voice cut through the din. Marquez stopped in mid-anecdote as he and his stunned admirers turned to see the most famous couple in wrestling. He was only tripped up for a moment before he found his stride.

"But, of course." He waved his minions away like so many peons and reached for Gabby's hand to kiss. "For the lady," he said, motioning to a barstool beside him. "And the greatest." He motioned for Gorpp to sit on the other side. "My attention is yours and it is undivided." Machete Marquez knew what opportunity knocking on your door looked like and this was it.

"We're here to offer you a job," Gabby said.

"I have a job," Marquez said with a wry smile.

"We're here to offer you a better job," she said.

"What does this better job pay?" he asked.

"Funny, you know," she looked at Gorpp. "I guess we never talked about that."

"There is no money on my world."

Marquez gave Gabby an, *is this guy serious* look. "You mean, your world up in the stars?" the masked man said pointing above him. Then he winked at a waitress who momentarily divided his attention.

"Yes," Gorpp said. "My world, up in the stars." He also pointed up.

Marquez looked back at Gabby the way a grownup would look to another grownup to translate whatever crazy thing their kid was saying.

"We're securing transportation to take the best in a professional wrestling ring to the rings of Saturn. The best. That's why we want you, Mr. Marqeuz."

Marquez looked around, like he expected the bartender or the party at the table next to them to affirm how crazy this all sounded.

"I don't know what's harder to believe, that you're taking a bunch of wrestlers on a spaceship to Saturn or that you expect them to do it for free."

Gorpp and Gabby didn't respond.

"Are you worried about your little secret getting out?"

"No one would believe you," Gorpp said.

"You got me there." Marquez looked around again, as if for help. "Listen, I will tell my father and his friends he plays dominoes and watches Lucha Libre with that I met the great Gorpp the Grappler and the amazing Firefly. They will be jealous. But I can't entertain crazy propositions." He patted Gabby's hand. "Come back when you have your spaceship. If I see that, I will do it for free! How about that?" With that, Marquez waved his groupies and hangers on back over to ogle him and buy him more drinks and laugh at his jokes and stories, none of which were half as crazy as the story he'd just heard.

Gorpp stepped over to a nearby table, made a few notes on a cocktail napkin to the effect that Marquez agreed to go on the tour in the event he was paid ten thousand dollars and shown proof of a "spaceship." Amid the giggles of the women surrounding Marquez, Gorpp handed him the napkin and pen. The laughter melted into an awkward quiet. Marquez read the napkin, took the pen and signed it with a flourish, then handed it back to Gorpp. "See you in the stars!" he said, then laughed. His fans laughed along with him, though they didn't really know what they were laughing at.

Gorpp reached into his pocket, pulled out ten thousand dollars in crisp bills and placed them on the bar in front of Marquez. "See you in space," he said, and now no one was laughing.

CHAPTER 8

NEXT ON THEIR list was "The Russian Blackbird." Dimitri Drozdov. And that meant a trip to Nikolaevsk, Alaska.

Nikolaevsk, in Russian, Никола́евск, is a small mostly ethnic Russian village in Alaska's Kenai Peninsula. Nikolaevsk's founders belonged to the Russian Orthodox Old-Rite Church. They call them Old Believers. Dimitri's family had been among the town's original settlers in 1968. And Dimitri Drozdov had been one of the great champions of wrestling all through the '70s. He was Gorpp's greatest rival, in the ring and, at times, out. He'd done some nasty turns to a few people in the business over the years but had mostly made amends, including with Gorpp.

Gorpp's vessel passed over Kachemak Bay State Park before touching down in a light snowfall in a wooded area just north of Fritz Creek. Gorpp's vessel allowed them to go to any climate on Earth in a matter of seconds, so they'd visited other cold places. Iceland, Antarctica, even the North Pole. But Gabby came from the south, she was a bible belt Georgia girl, not a Eastern Europe Georgia girl,, and she didn't have too much tolerance for cold. She knew how John White Eagle felt being in New York City, even in late April. When she thought about the cold on the moons of Saturn, a prickle of anxiety tingled her neck and back.

"How much farther?" she rasped, inhaling a gulp of frigid air. They tromped through ankle high snow, pushing frost-covered branches and brush out of their path until they found a trail that led to a homestead with a smoking chimney. Gabby looked for her old Mustang, that Gorpp had convinced her to give to Dimitri's nephew, but all they saw parked in front was an old Harley lowrider with ape hangers. Seemed an odd choice of transportation in these parts.

Dimitri's father answered the door of the cabin he'd built with his own hands in 1968. His white beard hung down below his waist. He wasn't accustomed to or welcoming to strangers. Particularly those as strange as Gorpp.

Gorpp could tell the old man knew who he was but that didn't incline him any more to hospitality. He told them Dimtri, and his nephew, Maxim, were ice fishing and pointed off in the direction of a nearby lake. As Gorpp and Gabby cleared the tree line, now wet with snow and ice, they spotted two figures in the middle of a clearing.

Gabby rubbed her mitten-covered hands on her thighs and chuffed out cold air that looked like smoke.

"I don't know anything about ice fishing, and I know this is Alaska, but doesn't it seem like it should be too warm for frozen over lakes you have to have an auger to drill into to fish in April?"

Gorpp looked at her but didn't respond. He often seemed to infer questions were rhetorical, even if they weren't.

As they got closer, the men sat facing them, watching them approach.

As graceful as she was, Gabby slipped a little and stumbled.

"You should have cleats on out here on the ice," Dimitri said.

"Don't even have snow boots," Maxim said to his uncle, as if the strangers weren't standing right in front of them.

"You need to pay proper respect, boy," Dimitri said to Maxim, with a glance to Gorpp and Gabby. "You're in the presence of two world champions."

"I already was in the presence of a world champion," Maxim said, not making eye contact with Gorpp or Gabby, but with a quick nod to his uncle.

After an uncomfortable silence, Gabby said, "You two look like hell. What happened to you?"

Uncle and nephew looked at each other, then Maxim looked again at the ground.

"Hey, we can't all be jetsetters, right? How's the famous couple doing, anyway?" Dimitri said.

Gabby decided to let it go for now, but the closer she looked at them the more she noticed fresh scars and scratches on their faces, and Dimitri was hunched over, favoring his left side.

She thought of why they'd come, and how absurd a proposition it seemed now, to invite Dimitri to be a headliner on professional wrestling's first interplanetary tour. Or anywhere for that matter. She wasn't sure he'd even be able to stand up from the looks of him.

Off on the edge of the lake, a branch cracked and then fell with a thud from the weight of the snow on it. It clawed at the pervasive silence like tearing paper.

After another awkward space in the conversation, Gabby tried to downshift to small talk and take another run at whatever this situation was they'd stumbled on up here in the woods, in Alaska. She rubbed her hands up and down on her arms, the tips of her fingers starting to feel numb, even with mittens.

"Anyway, is it really supposed to be so goddamn cold, in April?" she blurted out.

"This place is colder than other places," Dimitri said.

"This region, your town, what place?" Gabby said.

"This place." Dimitri pointed to the ice below his chair. He looked at Maxim, but his nephew still wouldn't look up. "Our place," he said.

Well, that just got even weirder, Gabby thought to herself. She looked at Gorpp for help, but he didn't respond. Gorpp was often content to let things unfold naturally. Gabby could get antsy and liked to nudge things along.

"Nephew, go to the house, get these two some cleats so they don't fall walking back, to wherever they came from. And bring her a proper jacket."

Maxim didn't look happy but he didn't hesitate to get up and start walking back to the house, in his snow boots and cleats. Once he was out of earshot, Dimitri, leaned toward them, wincing in pain, and said in an almost conspiratorial tone, "Tell me what you're doing here."

"We came to offer you a job, headlining the greatest tour in the history of wrestling, a tour of the stars. The stars of wrestling and the stars in the sky," Gabby said. "We came because we want you to come to Gorpp's home world, to a moon called Enceladus in the rings of Saturn. Dimitri, what happened to you?"

He looked around as if he expected a bogeyman to materialize from the ice. He spoke in hushed tones, wincing every few words. "Maxim is mixed up with, he calls it a motorcycle club, I call it a gang of hoodlums. According to their jackets, what they call 'cuts,' they call themselves the Kenai Henchman." He looked back toward the house. Maxim was still inside. "I thought I'd made it clear to, this club, that my nephew wasn't going to be a member anymore." He traced a fresh cut on his lip with his finger. "A half dozen of them came by yesterday. Apparently, I hadn't made it as clear as I'd thought."

"Jesus, Dimitri!" Gabby said. "Do you need help?"

"I can fight my own battles," he hissed at her but then

Maxim came out of the house with a bundle of supplies in his arms and Dimitri gave a quick nod 'no' to Gorpp and Gabby, making it clear that was the end of the conversation. Maxim tromped back over the ice and gave Gorpp and Gabby cleats they could put over their shoes, and an insulated fleece jacket for Gabby. She didn't feel much warmth from the men in the Drozdov family, but she burrowed into the jacket and felt a warm wave of gratitude for that. There was something downright unnerving about the cold here at the Drozdov homestead.

They said their goodbyes. Dimitri assured Gabby it was no problem to keep the jacket. They had plenty of jackets. Maxim never properly acknowledged Gorpp or Gabby. As they passed back by the motorcycle in the front yard, Gabby figured it was pretty obvious what had happened to her Mustang.

CHAPTER 9

On a supply run at a Homer market, Gabby picked up the latest issue of *World Wrestling Digest* and saw that her old rival, Coach Karla Becker, and Katie Camaro would be squaring off in a ladies headliner in Charlotte. Firefly was going to need someone to square off against so Charlotte was their next stop.

The match took place at the new Charlotte Amphitheater and Pavilion. USPW had bought out Hank Frizzel's Upland South territory a couple years back. Their production value was better. The new arena was definitely cleaner. And the wrestlers were the best of the best, but it just wasn't the same. To Gabby, all the matches, the spots and the storylines seemed too sanitized, too scripted. Too safe.

Gabby got waved through security when she went backstage to see the two top women in wrestling, so long as she wasn't competing herself. She found, to her astonishment, not only that there was a women's locker room but that they each had their own private dressing rooms. Maybe there was something to the USPW. She knocked on Coach Becker's door, heard laughing inside the room, then, "Come in!"

Katie Camaro was sitting on her supposed rival's couch,

unlacing her boots. She and Becker looked at Gabby and their faces showed their surprise. Gabby didn't know if they were expecting someone but they sure weren't expecting her.

"The Firefly has landed in Charlotte," Becker said to Camaro.

"May I come in?" Gabby asked.

"Be our guest," Becker said with a grand gesture and a touch of sarcasm in her voice.

"I'll just cut to the chase," Gabby said. "I'm here to hire you away from the USPW."

Camaro pulled a boot off with a grunt. "Do tell," she said. "But first, close that door."

Gabby ran through her usual spiel about the greatest stars going to the stars and the rest. As she talked, she noticed the body language between the two women and wasn't surprised when Becker responded the way she did.

"If we go, wherever we go, we're a package deal," she said.

Gabby quickly realized having the three of them would lend much better to a sustained storyline than just her and one other woman anyway. "You got it," she said.

Becker and Camaro left it that they wanted to sleep on it before they decided for sure but Gabby could tell how excited they were at the prospect, not just of traveling to the stars, but of not working for the USPW. They may have had their own dressing rooms, but Camaro's comment about how Hank Frizzel and Ernie Cantrell never leered at them the way the suits did now was telling.

CHAPTER 10

They were pretty much through with the one-on-one recruiting and ready to fill out the roster. They rented out the Omni in Atlanta on a Saturday when it was dark in early May and put an ad in the *Atlanta Journal Constitution* and the *Digest* and spread the word among the talkers in the business, like Steve Levey and Howie Shows. They set up a ring and a camera for promos and opened the doors at ten a.m. Their goal was to line up at least a dozen or so wrestlers who could work anywhere on the card.

They kept it vague about where the tour was going, most figured Japan or maybe Australia, and just tried to dazzle the good prospects with their celebrity and earnestness. It worked like a charm. They signed up some great hands including: old timer, "Iron Claw" Martinez who was coming out of retirement, again (a good foil for Machete Marquez); the Sarasota surfer, Wade "Big Wave" Rich; "The Puerto Rican Princes" Mia Camilla (that was four female wrestlers); "Lightning" Jackson from Dallas; "The Ugandan Giant" Makusa, who'd once nearly defeated Dimitri Drozdov in a tournament for the world title Gorpp had vacated; former FSU football star, and Heavyweight Championship

Wrestling's Florida champion, Willie Winston (along with his aunt, who insisted on coming along); and a handful of other wrestlers, referees, ring builders and other support staff.

That night, to celebrate, they went to The Sun Dial, a swanky revolving restaurant atop the tallest building in Atlanta, the Westin Peachtree Plaza. A seventy-three story cylinder of reflective glass, the plaza was a tourist attraction in and of itself and offered some of the most spectacular views of Atlanta anywhere. The couple enjoyed a quiet meal by candlelight as the sun set on downtown.

There were still a couple of loose ends. They needed to firm up with Bobby, but they felt confident, after today, he would be on board. They'd need to remember to lie to White Eagle about how cold it was gonna be on Enceladus, Gabby thought. And they needed to secure the ship. Gorpp had another prospect in mind but he would check on that when he went to Central Command. That just left one other stop before they left Earth's atmosphere, a visit home for Gabby and her husband, the alien, with Dr. and Mrs. Miller in Buckhead, there in Atlanta.

CHAPTER 11

GORPP TOUCHED down in the woods behind a nearby golf course in Buckhead for the visit with the in-laws before they took their big trip. They could have passed for any young married couple taking a lovely spring stroll through the upscale Atlanta suburb of Buckhead, if it weren't for Gorpp's oversized head, almond eyes and eggshell white body suit. They managed to skirt the golf course, and walk the couple remaining blocks in the neighborhood without attracting too much attention.

The Millers, and the landscapers, handymen, maids, and others they employed, kept the Miller residence always looking its best. Gabby rang the doorbell and could recognize her father's striding gait as the wood foyer creaked under his approaching steps. He unlocked and opened the big oak door.

The smile that touched his face the moment his eyes fell on his daughter made him look much more approachable. His shoulders relaxed, as though he'd been relieved of a wearisome burden. His baby girl was home. Safe. He reached out his hand to shake Gorpp's. Gabby had talked to Gorpp about this. Gorpp thought nothing of declining to shake hands and he mostly got away with it because he was Gorpp the Grappler. The greatest. But Gabby explained he had to shake her father's hand. He wasn't sure he understood why really, but he understood that the why didn't matter. What mattered was that it was important to her. So he shook Dr. Miller's hand. That awkward formality over with, Gabby's father embraced her in a big hug. "Welcome home, darling," he said.

"Who's at the door?" her mother called from somewhere in the big house.

"Come see, my sweet!"

"My sweet?" they heard her repeat back to herself and a moment later she stood at the entrance to the foyer and put her hands to her face in delighted surprise. "Oh, my baby," she said, and opened up her arms. Soon, both parents and Gabby were in a group hug. Gorpp stood to the side. Then they all let go at the same time.

"Come in, come in," Gabby's mother said, ushering them into her home. *Don't let 'em get away!* "I've got fresh-brewed ice tea and fresh-squeezed lemonade with lemons from our tree. Or you can go half and half.

"I'll have the half and half," Gabby said as they walked into a kitchen flooded in sunlight and gleaming clean. She looked at Gorpp. "He'll have the same."

"Will you be staying a while?" her dad couldn't help but blurt out.

"Well, daddy," Gabby said. "We're actually here to let you know we're going on a trip, for a while, a pretty long trip.

Her parents looked at each other. "You were right," her father said to her mother. Apparently they'd figured out on their own, or at least her mother had, they were going to go to Gorpp's home world one of these days. It seemed they both teared up at the same time.

"Oh, Jesus Christ," Gabby said. "Mom, dad, I'm sorry. We're coming back. We'll just be gone for, you know, probably the summer.

Her mother grabbed a clean dish towel and found a place on the clean counter that suddenly required her attention. Her father put a hand on his hip, turned and looked out at his garden through the window. He made a sound a couple times that sounded like, "Ayuh."

"It's pretty exciting, really," Gabby said with manufactured enthusiasm in her voice. "Can you imagine the stories we'll have when we come back?"

"Mmm," her mother said, scrubbing with intention now.

"Ayuh," her father said, back still turned to them.

"We're taking wrestling to Saturn! We're bringing Bobby, and Steve Levey's gonna call the matches. Howie Shows is gonna come and get the big story firsthand for *World Wrestling Digest*. John White Eagle too." When even White Eagle, who she knew her father respected, failed to get a reaction, she trailed off.

"You're standing in the kitchen where you grew up, Gabby, and telling your mother and me you're going to the planet, Saturn?" He sounded uncharacteristically petulant to her ear.

She looked at Gorpp. "Go ahead," she said.

"We'll actually be travelling to the planet's sixth-largest moon, what Earthlings call Enceladus."

"They have a Hilton there or are you staying with Gorpp's family?"

Another thing they hadn't really talked about.

"Our ship will have ample room to serve as long-term lodging," Gorpp said.

"Is it parked outside?" Dr. Miller asked.

"No, I haven't yet procured the one we will need for this trip."

"I see." He started to turn back to the window but steadied himself with a hand on the countertop instead. "Is it safe?" he asked Gorpp.

"Safety is relative," Gorpp answered.

At least he shook his hand, Gabby thought, cringing.

"Daddy, it's as safe as the trans-Atlantic cruise Aunt Gina took. Ok? And everybody was super excited about that."

"Fair enough," he said, resigned, as if you could be persuaded to just stop worrying. "Well, I hope it's a great trip, a safe trip. Send your old dad a postcard, huh?"

Everyone kept to safe topics over a homecooked dinner of Cornish hens, lima beans, greens cooked with a ham hock and another round of half and halfs. When they were leaving, Gabby's mother hugged Gorpp, he looked to Gabby for guidance and she motioned for him to hug her back, which he did, in his own awkward way.

When Gabby hugged her father, he whispered in her ear, "Don't forget that postcard."

"Ok, daddy."

Next up was the ship.

CHAPTER 12

THE LAST TIME Gorpp had been to Central Command was several years before, when he declared himself the Supreme Ruler and Champion of Earth and ordered his own kind to stand down their invasion. That had gone better than he'd anticipated, so he returned to the corridors of Central Command headquarters hopeful this more covert mission would also meet with success.

He was virtually invisible as he passed the many functionaries buzzing about the hive, as he once had. They wore the same clothes, had his same features but, now, lived a life he could no longer imagine. As expected, no one took much notice of him. Even if he were recognized, it's not like there was a warrant out for his arrest. That's not the way his culture worked. And it's why he thought stealing the ship should be easy. They didn't really have crime, so no efforts were expended to safeguard against it. But Gorpp had learned a few things from Earthlings, and from wrestling, things that would never occur to his kind.

As he stepped into the main hangar, huge ships hung suspended before him. It was like a showroom of the latest technology in space travel. He could just pick the one he wanted and take it for a test drive. He strolled along through the hangar, gawking at the immense vessels lined up before him, and he remembered one of the first training sessions he had before he shipped out for the invasion, or, as it turned out, interminable occupation, of Earth. The instructor introduced the human concepts of lying, theft, and deception. His memory was that they all, including the instructor, found the concepts so hard to conceive of, so alien, that they failed to afford them much consideration.

Gorpp stopped under the latest addition to the fleet, what we would crudely translate as the StarSail 9000. This was unquestionably the ship. He'd return to the small vessel docking port, pilot his little transport back here to stow away in the massive StarSail's hangar, then be off to pick up his passengers. He looked forward to the prospect of being at the helm of such a massive ship, and to testing out the latest refinements and upgrades in a real-world situation. But he had one stop to make first.

Having infiltrated human culture, or one aspect of it anyway, but not defecting permanently, like Gorpp, Overalls had been promoted in the hierarchy at Central Command. His workstation was close to the council meeting space. Gorpp didn't announce himself, just stood behind him until Overalls sensed his presence. It only took a moment, in their time.

"Why are you here?" came the question in Gorpp's mind. He'd grown so accustomed to verbal communication, it was jarring.

"I'm here to take you home."

Overalls turned to face him. Gorpp saw Overalls' mind light up at the thought of returning home. Gorpp told Overalls to come along on a walk with him so they could discuss it. He did. Overalls was so overwhelmed by the prospect of returning home after so long, he hardly noticed as he and Gorpp boarded Gorpp's two-person vessel, flew into the main hangar deck, stowed the vessel inside the hangar of the StarSail and made their way to the bridge to start activating the big ship's main control systems. It was as if Overalls wasn't making the connection. The promise of returning home wasn't hypothetical. He was participating in making it happen, even as they talked about it.

In just a few of their minutes the ship was ready to sail through the stars, no flight deck or air traffic control, no security. They just whooshed out of the hangar and into open space above Earth's atmosphere, then started descending rapidly toward Tampa where Gabby and Bobby had assembled everyone for the pick-up.

As the StarSail plunged down through the atmosphere, Overalls wondered aloud, in Gorpp's head, anyway, "where are we going?" It was a foggy sunrise in early May at the Bayfront Armory in Tampa. Gorpp brought the massive ship down close enough so commuters saw a strange turquoise glow in the fog above the bay that morning. Gorpp could look down at the parking lot, empty except for their passengers and their vehicles. He opened the receiving door at the bottom of the StarSail and engaged the energy beam that acted like an ethereal elevator to safely levitate the passengers from the confines of Earth's gravity to the climate- and gravity-controlled environment aboard the StarSail.

First he brought Gabby up. She arrived as if through a trap door, ensconced in a golden light. Once aboard, the glow faded and the floor reappeared beneath her. She grabbed Gorpp to hug him before she spoke.

"Is everything alright?" he asked, knowing it wasn't.

"Bobby got a message from Maxim that he's on the run, and he's afraid what will happen if the Kenai Henchmen find him. He asked Bobby to tell us he wants to go on the tour as Dimitri's son, Son of Blackbird. It sounds like he mainly wants to get as far away from this planet as possible."

Gorpp didn't respond.

"After we get everyone on board here can we pick him up?"

"Yes," Gorpp said.

He activated the ethereal elevator again and this time he brought Bobby on board. Howie Shows had been worried his flight in from JFK (he still thought of it as Idlewild) would be delayed but he was next on the elevator. He wouldn't miss a thing. Then came White Eagle.

"Hey, John," Gabby said. "Did you bring your sunglasses and swim trunks?"

White Eagle just looked around the massive spaceship in a kind of fog. Next was Coach Becker and Katie Camaro. They arrived on the elevator in an embrace and looked relieved to have the ground, or at least a floor, beneath them again. Gorpp and Gabby had wanted to bring everyone aboard they'd really explained things to first but there was one missing.

"Where's Levey?" Gabby said.

Gorpp didn't respond. How should he know? He was confident this was, in fact, a rhetorical question.

Bobby took charge. "Gorpp, we need you to go find Levey." He looked at Overalls. "Can you bring the rest of 'em up? We need all of 'em, including the referee, the ring builder, Winston's aunt with all the merchandise, all of 'em. And the equipment, from

the ring and lights and the popcorn machine, to boots and trunks and the box of razorblades. All of it."

Overalls didn't respond, but he went to the controller Gorpp had used and stood at the ready.

"Thank you," Bobby said. "Gabby, we need you to explain to all these people what's going on as soon as they get on board so we don't have a riot or some kind of mass hysteria on our hands. Got it?"

Gorpp turned to head for the hangar, and his own vessel,

for the quick trip to the Columbia Restaurant. The place he thought of as Steve Levey's domain.

Overalls had everyone and all of the equipment on board in a matter of minutes. And Gabby had her work cut out for her to maintain order.

"Ok, everybody, can I have your attention?" She briefly got the attention of a couple panicked wrestlers, but most were still zigzagging like zombies around the deck, trying to make sense of what had just happened to them and where they had been taken.

She clapped a couple times and tried again. "Please, may I have your attention?"

She looked at Overalls but he didn't respond. He'd completed the task that had been assigned to him.

She stepped up on a bulkhead and raised her voice. "Alright, knuckleheads, that's enough! I'm done treating you like babies. Is it news to anyone aboard that my husband isn't from around here?" She didn't see any hands. "I didn't think so. You're all big tough wrestlers, so here's the drill. For anyone wondering if we were flying coach to Sydney or Jonestown, I can tell you now, we're flying first class all the way to the rings of Saturn. If anyone isn't *on board* for that trip, say so now and Overalls here'll put you right back in the Armory parking lot, same way he brought you up. Last call if anyone's getting off." She looked around again. "Mr. Marquez?" She looked at the USPW sensation who had told them to their faces he didn't believe any of it was all real.

"I gave you my word, and my signature on a cocktail napkin. More importantly, I no longer have your ten thousand dollars, so fly me to the moon," Marquez said with a sarcastic Fred Astaire dance step.

Maybe they were in shock, or maybe the peer pressure not to appear weak prevailed, but once they were onboard the StarSail, not one of them took Gabby up on her offer to disembark.

"Alright, that's more like it. Listen to me, people, this trip we're about to take is going to make, not just wrestling history, and not just Earth history, but interstellar history. You are wrestling's Lewis and Clarks, and Sacagaweas, of the stars." She had their full attention now.

"Overalls, raise your hand." She pointed at him. "Overalls will show you to your quarters, give you a little tour of your new home, the StarSail 9000."

"Is that the ship's name, StarSail Nine Thousand?" John White Eagle asked.

Gabby looked at Overalls, then turned back to White Eagle. "I think that's more like, the model or manufacturer name, John. You know, like a Ford Mustang GT"

"Well, our ship should have a name."

"John White Eagle, you've just been appointed head of the ship naming committee. Anything else before we get you all settled in?"

She looked around the room but no one spoke up.

"We need to go to Nikolaevsk, get Maxim, and Dimitri, if we can, then we can come back and check on Steve," Gabby said.

"That doesn't make sense," said Marquez from the back of the room, leaning like James Dean against the wall. "We're already in Tampa."

Overalls touched a few buttons. "We are now in Nikolaevsk, Alaska."

Gabby relished the flash of shock in Marquez's eyes. He wasn't used to getting outfoxed, much less in such a public way.

Bobby and Marquez took the ethereal elevator down to a clearing just west of the lake where Gorpp and Gabby had last seen Maxim and Dimitri. Gabby stayed onboard with Overalls to keep the villagers from getting restless.

Bobby saw the smoke from the Drozdovs' chimney and

they made for it. They'd only just started out when they heard the rumble of an engine a ways off.

"Think that's Maxim?"

"Or the Henchmen," said Marquez.

"If it was the Henchmen, there would be more than one engine," Bobby said.

"You're right."

Within a few minutes of sloshing through the underbrush, covered in places by ice with snow mounds along the way, they made it to the front door of the cabin. The motorcycle was gone and they saw fresh skid marks in the snow. Bobby gave a firm knock, more of a pounding on the door, and shouted, "Hello!" No response.

Marquez grabbed the doorknob, found the door unlocked and strode into the sparse and tidy Drozdov living room, a small fire crackled in the fireplace. Bobby hesitated, then followed. "Hello!" Bobby called out again. It sounded much louder inside the quiet of the cabin than it had in the expanse of outside. Still no response. They could feel the place was empty.

"There's a note," Bobby said, picking up a piece of paper he found on the mantle.

"I'm on the run. Find me. --M," Bobby read aloud, then looked up.

They quickly agreed the best bet was to get back to the ship, locate him with radar and grab him up through the ethereal elevator so they returned. They tracked melting snow and mud on the pristine floors of the StarSail as they made their way to find Gabby and Overalls. Overalls entered information into the ship's AI and within a few moments they had a visual image, from above, of Maxim. He must have been going over a hundred miles an hour, sending snow flying out from behind his bike as he raced down the highway.

Overalls made a few minor adjustments in their position,

matched Maxim's speed and almost instantly they were right above him. He activated the ethereal elevator and Maxim appeared in the center of the room, still on his motorcycle and still traveling at high speed. Overalls made a split second adjustment that minimized the impact as Maxim and his Harley collided with a bulkhead and then the wall. The bike lay on its side, engine still grumbling like a wounded bear, black smoke pouring from the exhaust and filling the room with the smell of burning gasoline. Marquez moved to kill the engine, but one look from Maxim made it clear, touching his bike wouldn't be a good idea. Maxim dragged himself to the ignition and pulled the key, leaving the room suddenly quiet after a few more belches of smoke and a backfire.

"Welcome aboard," Gabby said with a look at White Eagle who'd come, along with several others, when they heard the motorcycle crash on the deck.

"To hell with the Henchman!" Maxim yelled, still sitting on the floor, clutching his ribs. His voice croaked from the cold air he'd been breathing just a moment before, and from the impact on his ribs when he crashed into the interior wall of the StarSail. It sounded like the kind of thing he expected the group to yell back but the room was silent.

"Long live the Ring Raiders!" he yelled, pumping a fist in the air with a wince of pain.

"Long live the Ring Raiders!" Overalls shouted back. Gabby and a few others looked at him quizzically.

Maxim then struggled to his feet, took a pocketknife from his belt and proceeded to pick at the Kenai Henchman patch on the back of his jacket until he'd loosened a corner enough to get a good hold of it and tear it off. He threw it on the floor, stomped on it and then spat on it. Then he went to work removing the bottom, Alaska, patch and finally the large patch in the center with a motorcycle-riding skeleton on an outline of Alaska.

Gabby was just about to inquire of Maxim about the safety

of Dimitri and the rest of their family when Gorpp appeared in a doorway and all eyes turned to him. He'd returned from his trip to the Columbia Restaurant in Ybor City and traveled to Alaska almost as fast as the StarSail. He looked at Gabby. "The restaurant wasn't open. I spoke to men in white aprons removing waste, in the back alley. They said Steve Levey had a stroke or heart attack last night at the bar. They said he spoke of going to the heavens all night, so they think he knew he would have the heart attack. He was taken by ambulance to Tampa General Hospital." Gorpp paused, then added, "I was going to ask him for another cigar."

"Overalls, take us back to Tampa," she said.

He pushed a couple buttons and nodded to affirm they were back.

Then a light on the control panel started flashing.

Gorpp and Overalls both rushed to it, then Gorpp looked back to Gabby.

"Central Command figured out I took the StarSail sooner than I'd anticipated, and they're sending reconnaissance."

"What does that mean?"

"It means, if they catch us they'll stop us from going," Gorpp said.

"That can't happen," said Overalls, then he pulled a lever on the console and the StarSail accelerated at a speed unimagined previously by our kind. The stars melted into a blur as did the consciousnesses of the humans onboard. Gorpp and Overalls had experienced comparable speeds before and got their senses back more quickly than ever thanks to the smooth ride of the StarSail 9000.

After a while, days for most, things started to settle back into place. Even such tremendous speed eventually becomes the new normal and internal systems start to reset.

Gabby sat in the observatory in a reclining chair ergonomically designed for a slightly different skeletal structure. As she looked at the solar system passing her by, she weighed the events that took place just before Overalls pulled that lever that catapulted them toward Saturn, away from their pursuers, and away from Steve Levey lying in a hospital bed at Tampa General, his dream of going to the stars having gone up in smoke.

Overalls' action couldn't be seen as insubordination since all he did was set them off on their charted course. She just couldn't bear the thought of having left Levey behind with no time taken for consideration, much less a visit, a card, some proper acknowledgement of regret before the show goes on. Speeding off like that didn't comport with her sense of basic southern hospitality, or good business, especially not with such a respected elder statesman. A hall of famer to be sure. It felt to her like one of those things in life you have to just sit with for a while, because you can't do anything to fix it.

They were two Earth-days out and most were still wandering around in a daze, like they were sedated by more than they could process. It kept the ship quiet.

Gorpp and Overalls monitored the controls though the ship mostly ran on auto-pilot. Gorpp could see a kind of smile curling up in Overalls' mind and he sent curiosity back into Overalls thoughts.

"I buzzed Tampa General on our way out of town," Overalls said.

"What does that mean?"

"It means everyone not in a coma or anesthetized at that hospital knows we passed by." And again, the hint of a smile. But something was holding it back.

"I sense something is concerning you," Gorpp said.

Overalls pointed to their radar detector. "They're gaining on us," he said.

"How is that possible?" Gorpp asked. "The StarSail 9000 was the fastest ship in the hanger."

"Maybe the ship pursuing us wasn't in the hangar," Overalls said.

Gorpp was beginning to think perhaps Central Command had adapted, familiarized themselves more with humans, become more Machiavellian than he had given them credit for, and it worried him.

Due to both Earth's and Saturn's elliptical orbits it was hard to say the exact distance between the two, but Gorpp figured it was close to eight hundred million miles. That was a long way to go with their pursuers gaining.

CHAPTER 13

GABBY FELT like the cobwebs were finally starting to clear. She wasn't sure how long she'd been on the ship. From the creak of her bones and the crick in her neck as she climbed out of the recliner on the observation deck, it felt like a good while. Gabby traversed the corridors of the StarSail and didn't see another soul. Didn't hear a sound but the quiet buzz of the ship's engines and central air. There were signs with symbols on them she didn't understand. She assumed they mostly said mundane things like CARGO HOLD or MESS HALL.

She rounded a corner and stopped when she saw a figure approaching. She wondered, for a moment, if it was an apparition. But as the figure got closer, she recognized the trench coat and scarf.

"It's cold on this ship," White Eagle said.

"I'm sorry," Gabby said. "I'll check with the boys and see if we can adjust the thermostat."

"I've been thinking about it, and I don't understand how it's going to be warm where we're going either."

"It's not, John."

"But you said--"

"I know what I said."

"Why would you, I mean--"

"Hey, asses in the stands, right? You've been in this business long enough. You shouldn't have been such an easy mark. I told you what I needed to, to get you on the ship."

"I guess you're right," he said. "Funny that you were telling the truth about the spaceship part. You just worked me on the weather." Then, wraith-like, he wandered on down the corridor. No updates from the ship-naming committee.

Gabby kept walking too. Getting her blood circulating and her heartrate up helped with the remaining cobwebs. And there seemed no end to the corridors she hadn't yet been down. The ship was a blend of muted eggshell white and silver, like Gorpp's uniform, elegant in design, but function was clearly prioritized over aesthetic.

Down a long corridor, Gabby saw a huddled form against the wall. As she neared, the hunched form of an old man came into focus. He was scribbling something on a notepad. Tufts of white hair puffed out on the sides of his otherwise bald head. Howie Shows. He startled her when he looked up and nearly shouted.

"Miss Miller!"

"That's Mrs.," she snapped back.

He looked down, *mea culpa* written on his drooping features.

"Mrs. Miller. It is Miller still, right?"

"That's right."

"You know, I was going to ask you something else for my article, but now I want to ask why you didn't you take Gorpp's last name. Does he have one? Or is Gorpp his last name?"

"We wouldn't be able to pronounce it."

"So you stuck with Miller."

"That's right. What was it you originally wanted to ask?"

"Oh, yes." He held his pencil up, as if in triumph. "What are Gorpp's people, his kind, what are they called?"

"The way he's tried to explain it to me, he feels the English word it would most closely translate to is human."

"Human?"

"Yes, he said, like humans, his people are bipedal and have large, complex brains. He said they are to his world as we are to ours in terms of analogous roles, recognizing how much more advanced they are than we probably ever will be."

"Well, none of that gobbledygook is what my readers want to hear. How about Saturnarians?"

"Howie, it's your magazine. I guess you can name them whatever you want."

"Saturnarians it is!"

Gabby gave him a friendly pat on the shoulder and continued on her way but Howie called out to her from behind.

"One more question. Have you named the ship yet?"

"That's White Eagle's department," she said. "Talk to him."

"*StarSail* it is!"

She found her way to the bridge and stood and watched Gorpp and Overalls, the Saturnarians, stare at screens and flashing lights, occasionally pushing a button or two. They reminded her of two boys playing Atari. They seemed oblivious of her.

"Hey, fellas," she said. "One of our guests asked if we could make it a little warmer on the ship. Got a button for that on your fancy console there?"

Gorpp looked at her. "White Eagle," he said.

"You got it."

She held his gaze and he broke away from what he'd been doing and came to her, embraced her. She hugged him back.

"How long have I been, you know—"

"In Earth-time, we departed just over fifty-two hours ago."

"Two days?"

"Two days, four hours."

"How come I'm not starving?"

"Your daily nutritional requirements are being provided through what you would call the HVAC or life support systems on the ship."

"What do you mean, like you're pumping microscopic infusions of spaghetti through the AC vents?"

"In a manner of speaking. It's an aerosolized vitamin-rich dietary supplement."

"Is that what you guys are eating?"

"Yes."

"Well, how efficient of you. Wait a second, what about going to the bathroom?"

"Not necessary," Overalls said. "The system also extracts waste from your body in much the same way, the way an air conditioning system also dehumidifies."

Gabby didn't know what to say to that.

The console started flashing again. Gorpp returned to the controls.

"What's happening?" she asked.

"They're closing the gap," Overalls said.

"How long before they catch up with us?"

"There are a few variables that make it difficult to know precisely but the relevant point is that it will be long before we reach home."

Gabby heard noise from somewhere in the ship, what sounded like banging. Gorpp and Overalls were focused on their radar system and didn't seem aware of it or concerned about it if they heard it. She decided to investigate. They didn't seem to notice when she left the control room.

She followed the rhythmic banging as she walked down the corridor and it got louder as she went. It stopped periodically, then started up again. She followed. She rounded a corner and saw a door standing open. She approached with caution but peeked into the open doorway.

What she saw was Hank, the ring builder, standing up on the apron of the wrestling ring they'd brought with them, with his back to her. He was tightening up one of the turnbuckles. He had almost finished assembling the entire ring.

"Hey, Hank. Whatcha doing?" She walked toward him.

"Hey there, Firefly! Well, I reckon I'm doing what y'all hired me on for, right?"

"Right. Well, I mean, we were going to have you build the ring once we arrived at our destination."

"Not Melbourne or Morocco, right?"

"Right."

"I understand that," Hank said. "I just, well, it's a long trip to 'not Melbourne or Morocco' and we got a bunch of wrestlers onboard and I just figured, I don't know, maybe they'd want something to do."

Gabby smiled. "That's very thoughtful of you, Hank. Thank you."

"You're welcome." He looked downright proud of himself. "Miss Firefly, do you think I could get a picture or an autograph from you?"

She smiled again. "First of all, it's Mrs., not Ms."

"Oh, right. Sorry."

"It's ok. And second, when we get to 'not Melbourne or Morocco' they're probably gonna want your picture and autograph."

"You think?"

"Honestly, Hank, I don't know what to think. This is a crazy adventure we've all signed up for. But where we're going they won't ever have seen anyone like us before so we'll all be celebrities there. Aliens!"

"Wow," Hank said. "I never thought about that."

CHAPTER 14

"WHY DO the Kenai Henchmen wish you harm?" Gorpp asked. They were seated in a small meeting room, across a table from Maxim. It reminded Gabby of interrogation scenes in cop shows like *Kojak* and *Rockford Files*.

"My uncle already told you," Maxim practically spat in his strong Russian accent. He refused to make eye contact and slumped in his chair, like a sullen brat, Gabby thought.

"Did they threaten you?"

Maxim didn't answer and he didn't look up but it wasn't long before the weight of the silence became more and more his burden, and not his interrogator's. He spoke almost in a whisper, as if he were ashamed.

"They came out and surrounded us on the lake, when we were fishing. Said they had dynamite and they'd blow up the lake and watch us freeze to death or drown if they ever caught either of us in the Kenai Peninsula again."

"Is your only interest in our tour to escape harm on Earth?" Gorpp asked.

Maxim just sulked. Then, as if it burst out of him, "My family founded Никола́евск!"

"Do you even know how to wrestle?"

This earned Gorpp a look of disdain from Maxim. "I've been wrestling with my uncle my entire life," he said. "I don't just know how to wrestle." He pointed at his head. *Smart guy.* "I know how to win."

"What does Dimitri think about this Son of Blackbird idea?" Gabby asked. "Do you even know where he is or if he's safe."

Maxim looked away again.

"Are you worried about your uncle?" Gabby asked. "Being left behind and all?"

"My uncle can take care of himself! And I'm not the one who left him behind. What about you? Am I some kind of prisoner here? Don't I have like diplomatic immunity or something under the Geneva Convention? I know my rights." With that, Maxim pushed his chair back so hard it fell over backwards, then he stomped off and slammed the door behind him, to the extent the hydraulics would allow.

"Son of Blackbird could work," Gorpp offered.

"Oh, the gimmick isn't the problem. I'm sure he can wrestle too. I just don't trust him. I think he's smarter than he lets on and I don't think he's being honest. I mean, did you buy any of that diplomatic immunity word soup bullshit? I sure didn't."

"Best thing is to keep him busy, not disconnected and in the shadows," Gorpp said.

"Keep your enemies closer?" Gabby said.

Gorpp didn't respond.

"Old Earth saying," she said.

When Gorpp didn't see the need he didn't respond, no matter how many prompts he got to do so.

"Son of Blackbird it is!" Gabby said. "Howie's gonna love it. From the father-son angle right down to the Harley." She smacked Gorpp's shoulder playfully. *Lightbulb!* "We could play 'Hell Bent for Leather' as he rides that rumbling motorcycle to the ring! Don't you love it?"

Gorpp didn't respond. But she thought about how funny it would be if, one day, he did respond to one of her *Don't you love it?* kind of questions.

"He'll put asses in the stands," Gorpp said, and there was that glint in the eye.

"Yes he will." She smiled, but it melted quickly from her features. "It's just dangerous to put someone on the tour, in the ring, that we don't trust. You know that."

"I know anything can be dangerous. And I don't know who I can trust, other than you and Bobby."

"What about Overalls? What about White Eagle?"

"Sometimes it's not about treachery but just a different lens or measure of values. By trust, I meant not just honor but also loyalty."

She turned to him and held his hands in hers. "Can I talk to you about something else?"

"Yes."

"We need to figure out who's going to fill in for Levey. It's an important role. There are a few candidates I could make a case for but I've landed back where I started when we first talked about this crazy idea. I think it's Overalls. He's the only one, other than you, who knows anything about your culture and ours. He'll be able to relate more to the home crowd. Don't you think?"

"I don't think it will work the way you're imagining but I will talk to him about it."

"What's not going to work the way I'm imagining, smartass?"

"My people communicate non-verbally, telepathically. They won't need a Steve Levey or Overalls telling them what's happening in the ring, or what to think about it."

"I think you're wrong," she said. "I think the right announcer can make or break this tour, and with Levey at home, hopefully recuperating, if heartbroken, we need to figure out who will bring the most to the table in his place. We might want to have White Eagle or maybe Howie do some color commentating but I think Overalls is our announcer, our anchor. He's the conduit to the crowd."

Then, the ship rocked so violently, Gabby was thrown to the floor, and even Gorpp had to hold onto the table to steady himself.

He helped her up, hugged her and whispered in her ear, "We are under attack."

On his way to the bridge he started to pick up on the thoughts of their pursuers from Central Command. They must be close. The thoughts felt like colors swimming in the stream of his subconscious. Thoughts of surprise, confusion, excitement, jealousy. It wasn't a very united front. Then he felt Overalls' stream of surprise, embarrassment, fright and then resolve.

Gorpp and Gabby hurried past confused wrestlers wandering the corridors. On the bridge, they found Overalls, Bobby and White Eagle staring at the viewfinder. In it, they saw another ship, sitting still, as they now were, beside them. Gorpp and Overalls recognized it as *Saturnarian* but had never seen it, or its like, before.

"What did they shoot at us?" Gabby said, with a crack in her voice she'd thought she could control. Fear she'd intended to mask, shone through.

"They didn't fire at us," Overalls said. "Their ship has no weapons."

It's not *Battlestar Galactica* or *Star Wars* out here, the way humans think, Gorpp thought. Overalls heard him.

"Well, something crashed into the ship," Gabby said. "It knocked me out of my chair."

"Nothing crashed into the ship. We encountered an energy field of kinds, generated by our pursuers." Overalls looked away from the screen and at Gabby. "They don't intend us harm. They just don't want us to go to our home world."

"So they zapped into existence some kind of high tech electrical wall we can't pass through? That's their big plan?"

Tough one, Gorpp thought. Could go either way on whether or not this question was rhetorical. Gorpp and Overalls didn't respond.

"Why don't they want us to go to your home world?" White Eagle asked Gorpp and Overalls.

"Because humans are chaotic," Overalls said.

"And we're an orderly people," Gorpp said.

"And humans are violent," Overalls said.

"Those are some pretty high horses, you're riding there, the both of you. Couple of hypocrites. You were on Earth to take it over, to take it from us, to what, eradicate us?"

Bobby looked at White Eagle and shook his head in resignation.

It's more complicated than that, Gorpp thought, reflexively, but didn't say.

It is and it isn't, he heard Overalls' thoughts in response.

"You can hear their thoughts already, can't you?" White Eagle said. "And each other's."

"Yes," Gorpp said.

"Let's invite them over," Gabby said, and all eyes turned to her.

"Asses in the stands," Bobby said. "That's brilliant. Most of us aren't telepaths, or whatever. We can't sell 'em on our show if we can't show 'em a promo. So, yeah. Let's have 'em over. If Steve was here, he'd wine and dine 'em and have 'em all smoking Cuban cigars. Hank's already got the ring built. We got a bunch of stir crazy wrestlers wandering the halls like zombies. Give 'em something to do. Let 'em earn their freight. Let's have some company."

CHAPTER 15

GABBY'S first impression watching them file in was that this is what it would be like if she went to Gorpp's family's house for dinner. They all looked like her husband. They were about the same height. They wore the same glittery, eggshell white suits. Then one of them stepped into her view and Gabby found herself in the presence, for the first time, of a female of Gorpp's kind. A hot flash of jealousy made her blush. She didn't have to be a telepath to see that it didn't go unnoticed by the female from the delegation, or Gorpp. How embarrassing, she thought.

It took her a moment to realize the delegation had been communicating with Gorpp and Overalls non-verbally since they stepped through the airlock, or maybe even before. There were five of them. One appeared to be in charge, the female and one other were maybe lieutenants, and there were two others who hung back. Were they security?

"Welcome aboard!" Gabby said, a little too loud, on purpose.

All the members of the delegation winced and covered their ears.

"Sorry," she said. (She wasn't). "I know you're not used to

our primitive way of communicating, but hey, it's rude to whisper, right? So, let's keep it verbal, shall we?"

The delegation looked around. She picked up on their sense of disorientation and distaste. Sometimes taking the low ground leveled the playing field. Something Bobby taught her when she first got into the wrestling business.

Despite her petulance, Gabby's instinct was to usher company in for a big meal around the dining room table, with fresh cut flowers as a centerpiece. But these weirdos got their nutrient particles from the air and there were no fresh cut flowers for millions of miles, so they brought them straight to the ring.

It was the longest ring walk in Gabby's career. Not being able to receive their mental transmissions but still knowing they were happening felt like a dream you can't remember but you still have the aftertaste from when you wake up. She reached out and held Gorpp's hand. She told herself it was because she wanted to see if any of the thought transmissions he was sending and receiving would seep into her consciousness, but she also didn't mind if the female delegation member took note.

Since they'd been a couple, Gabby had pressed Gorpp a few times for more information about his people, his world, their culture and customs, but he was always cagey and evasive. She realized she didn't even know what their societal perceptions of beauty were or if they paired off in monogamous relationships. The weight of what she didn't know pressed down on her.

Bobby and White Eagle waited like ushers outside their makeshift wrestling arena in space. They welcomed the delegation with wide eyes. Their guests entered the large space to find all the lights dimmed except those above the ring. The way they stared at the contraption reminded Gabby of little kids at Christmas more amazed by the box than the gift inside.

Like a studio taping, they only had a handful of seats and spectators for tonight's card, but they'd assembled everyone on board who wasn't wrestling to be in the audience. There were five empty chairs in the front row. Bobby and White Eagle ushered their guests to the front row for the first ever Heavyweight Championship Wrestling event in space.

As soon as they were seated, Overalls, wearing a Steve Levey lookalike suit he and Gabby cobbled together, stepped from the apron through the ropes and into center ring. Hank, in the back of the room, killed all the lights except the one on Overalls as a microphone lowered from the ceiling.

"Ladies and gentlemen, welcome to the StarSail 9000 Arena, where tonight, you will be witness to the first ever professional wrestling matches in space!"

White Eagle leaned in close and whispered to Gabby. She thought he was going to make a remark about naming the ship, but instead he said, "Kind of gives new meaning to 'space opera,' huh?"

Gabby offered the obligatory smile, but she was trying to get a good look at the delegation in the dim light. She saw Howie sitting cross-legged on the floor, scribbling furiously in his notepad.

The roar of an engine from outside the room caused all eyes to turn to the doorway just in time to see Maxim rumble in on his Harley as gas fumes filled the air. He parked the bike at ringside and climbed in the ring, yanking the microphone away from a stunned-looking Overalls (though it was all scripted out by Gorpp, Gabby and Bobby ahead of time).

Maxim had on wrestling boots and trunks but also his leather vest, now devoid of patches, along with a helmet and wraparound sunglasses that reminded Gabby of Duck from the Conch Republic. Maxim ceremoniously removed his helmet and shoved it into Overalls' stomach. Overalls held onto it as if somehow he had been conscripted to be Maxim's valet. Next Maxim took off his sunglasses and handed those to Overalls too. When he spoke into the mic it was barely more than a seething whisper. He looked directly at the head of the delegation.

"We're here to deliver a message," Maxim said, pointing at them. "Tell your people we're coming for them. We're coming for your world. Are you scared of us?" Raising his voice now. "You're right to be scared. We are your conquerors!" He lowered the mic then and just looked at them and laughed. Then, Maxim shouted, "To hell with the Kenai Henchman!"

"To hell!" the crowd behind Gorpp's people bellowed back.

"Long live the Ring Raiders!" he shouted.

"Long live!" came the answer back.

The delegation were looking all around, not sure what was happening.

Hank flickered the lights on and off throughout the room, then he turned the house lights all the way up. All eyes followed Maxim as he looked down to see Gorpp leaning on the seat of his Harley. He raised the mic back to his mouth.

"You're gonna want to step away from my bike," he said to Gorpp.

Gorpp didn't move.

"Last warning."

Gorpp didn't even bother looking up.

Maxim pushed the mic away and charged across the ring before diving over the top rope. Gorpp moved just in time and Maxim crashed into his bike, sending it tumbling to the ground in a screech and crunch of metal, bone and flesh. Before he could scramble to his feet, Gorpp was on him, reigning blows down on his head, shoulders and back.

Machete Marquez and Makusa, the Ugandan Giant, rushed to Maxim's rescue. Makusa peeled Gorpp off of Maxim like he weighed less than a fly. He held him in a full nelson as Marquez delivered tomahawk chops that sent

Gorpp's head reeling. With the house lights up, Gabby could see the delegation were enthralled, and horrified.

Marquez and the crowd got into a rhythm where between each chop, they would all shout, "Long live!" Overalls motioned frantically to one of the hands at ringside and he started ringing the bell but the chops and chants continued.

On cue, Gabby and Overalls converged on the delegation. Gabby knew Overalls was communicating to them that he was afraid the crowd would turn on the delegation next and that we needed to evacuate them from the room for their safety. They quickly followed as Overalls and Gabby ushered them out amid the chopping and chanting and rushed them into the small meeting room where Gorpp and Gabby had interviewed Maxim.

As soon as the delegation was secured, Overalls and Gabby stepped back out into the corridor. He pulled her in close so he could speak softly.

"It's working," he said. "They are overloaded with confusion, panic and a kind of visceral attraction and revulsion."

"Asses in the stands," she said.

"I have to get to the bridge," he said.

"Wait," Gabby said. "Do you think, you know –" she gestured to the door. "Do you think she's attractive?"

"Yes," he said, then turned and made his way to the bridge to execute the most important part of their plan.

Before Gabby could respond, Gorpp rounded the corner with Bobby and White Eagle right behind him.

"Are we ready?" Gorpp asked.

"He just went to the bridge," Gabby said.

Gorpp looked at Bobby, who nodded, and opened the door. As it opened, the chants of "Long live!" could still be heard from outside the room. They went in and faced the delegation with the stern expressions of serious men. Gorpp felt the feintest lurch and knew their plan was working.

"We have a very serious situation on our hands" he said, way too loud. The Saturnarians' hands went back over their ears. Gorpp continued speaking, not just aloud, but loud. "I had no idea of the danger this human posed until now," he lied, and he sold it like a professional wrestler at the height of his talents.

The urgent thoughts that came streaming back made clear their attention was no longer on the force field and, almost instantly, he felt the ship break free. Then the female in the delegation snapped out of it and realized what Gorpp had done.

"They've broken through!" She said it aloud, and also loud, as if to drown out Gorpp's blather. All of them focused and realized what happened, but they were less clear on why. With their concentration broken, the energy net they'd erected, by harnessing both their mental energy and that of their ship, had been weakened enough for the StarSail to sail through it.

"You're our guests now," Gorpp said. "Enjoy your stay on the StarSail 9000."

They didn't respond.

Gorpp and his human companions left the room. Once in the corridor, Gabby turned to Gorpp and stopped him.

"So it worked?"

"Yes," he said. We're underway again."

"Are we, I mean, are we holding them hostage?"

"No," he said. "They can return to their ship whenever they choose. It's following us again, of course."

"Couldn't they put up another force field, or whatever?"

"I suppose they could, but I don't think they will."

"Why not?"

"They're deeply confused and disoriented and, remember, time moves much slower for them. It may not even occur to them to leave that room until after we've arrived."

"So I guess our plan worked. I didn't think about them staying on board."

"Our plan worked and we are nearing Jupiter. Soon we will arrive at Enceladus."

"And make wrestling history!" said Howie Shows who'd been eavesdropping behind them and frantically scribbling in his pad.

CHAPTER 16

THE WRESTLERS HAD COME to refer to the malaise of the first leg of their journey, when they were all adjusting to highspeed space travel, as the "space zombies." As in, this guy's got a case of the space zombies. What they had come to think of as the second leg was once they got wind they were being chased. Most on board didn't really make the connection of how the show they staged led to them being able to keep going, but it did, and a wrestling explanation was good enough to boost morale to a new high.

Gorpp found it interesting how even veteran wrestlers like John White Eagle could be made so easily into marks.

Coach Becker and Katie Camaro decided a celebration was in order. They consulted with Overalls and learned that any material items they wanted, from food to fine art to Steve Levey's suit, could be recreated onboard almost immediately in most cases. They didn't understand how but were grateful for the technology. What they envisioned as a cast party ended up feeling like a high school dance for misfits.

They decorated the same large room where the match took place, with the ring still as the centerpiece, in the same way

Gabby's mom would use those fresh cut flowers as the centerpiece on the dining room table. The theme, of course, was space! They used paint and sharpies to make signs on poster board and a big roll of butcher paper with slogans like: "The invasion has started!" and " Saturn, you're next!" It struck the right chord with a room full of wrestlers not used to feeling like zombies or like they were running from something, running scared.

Howie wrote an article for the *Digest* about Maxim's declaration of war against Saturn and the ensuing mele with Gorpp, the evacuation. He felt compelled to opine with a sense of loftiness and dignity, as if he were writing the official history, not a splash piece for a wrestling magazine. Though there wouldn't be anybody to read it until they returned, except for those onboard.

The jubilance of that time was short-lived. They were about to pass the Eye of Jupiter.

Gabby couldn't make sense of not even noticing, or remembering if she did, when they'd passed Mars. After all the old B-movies and science fiction novels and tabloid stories about Martians, you'd have thought it would be the talk of the ship, but now they were long past the red planet, and she had no memory of even catching a glimpse. Had she slept through it like a child at the late movie?

Now they were right beside the unblinking Eye of Jupiter. Gorpp and Gabby stood side by side on the observation deck. The red eye stared back at them.

"What is it?"

"It's a storm," Gorpp said. "It's been going on for hundreds of Earth years."

"One storm?"

"One of many. The biggest."

"Like a hurricane?"

"Much stronger than your hurricanes." Gabby didn't know if it was conscious, but she felt like she was hearing more "yours" in Gorpp's descriptions of Earth as they got closer to his home world.

"How big is it?"

"About three times bigger than Earth."

"The storm is three times bigger than Earth?"

"Yes."

"Why does that make me want to cry?" Gabby asked, sounding as if she may already be crying.

Gorpp looked at her and then led her gently by the arm away from the observation area to seats in the middle of the deck that he quickly turned away from the windows and observation monitors. Gabby was openly weeping now. He held her to his shoulder and gently stroked her hair.

"Why?" she asked again, forcefully through the tears.

"It's similar to what happened to you and the others when we first departed. Your system needed time to adjust to high speed space travel. Being in the presence of Jupiter, it's straining your consciousness, your identity. Humans think of themselves as being at the center of the universe, perhaps the only things in the universe. Just the Eye of Jupiter is three times the size of Earth, the planet itself is eleven times the size of your world. It's a human fragility that your psyche has to wrestle with to recalibrate."

"Human fragility? You can be so high and mighty sometimes. Are *your* people just too advanced to have feelings, is that it?"

"We, of course, learned through experience about the emotional challenges of space travel, over time, and adapted."

"Well, why didn't you warn us about any of this? Warn *me*?" She gave him a spirited but good-natured, punch on the arm, then wiped her tears with the back of her sleeve like she did as a little girl.

"What good would it have done you to anticipate these feelings in advance?"

"I don't know," she said. "I just think it would do me

some good for you to anticipate my feelings in general, you know?" Gabby got up and walked off the observation deck.

CHAPTER 17

THAT EVENING, Gabby took a shower long enough to steam up the whole bathroom in their quarters, even with the StarSail 9000's advanced dehumidification systems. She felt herself staving off another malaise as they neared Saturn. The further she got from Earth, the more she felt unmoored. It was a struggle to make herself do basic things like shave her legs in the shower. What was the point? Gabby wrapped one white towel around her midriff and another around her hair and came out into their living quarters with a cloud of steam around her. Gorpp sat with his perfect posture, staring out at space, stars passing by them on the way back to his home. He didn't acknowledge her as she puttered about. Her ballerina music box on the mantle was one of the only reminders of home for Gabby in their living quarters. She opened it and listened the melody she's heard since she was a little girl, growing up in Buckhead. After a few minutes, she came and sat beside him, looking out at the stars herself.

"They still haven't come out, you know. How long has it been?"

"They're thinking," he said. "Time moves more slowly for them and we gave them a lot to consider." She'd heard it all before. She turned to face him but he kept looking straight ahead.

"Did it ever occur to you that maybe your big invasion wouldn't have worked? That we would have won?"

"No."

"Oh yeah, and why not?"

"That's a very Earthnocentric point of view," he said.

"Uhh," she more groaned than said. "The arrogance. You thought becoming the champion of wrestling would mean you were champion of Earth. And this, delegation, or whatever they are, they saw a pretty typical show for us and it's put them into some kind of stupor or hibernation."

"It wouldn't have happened the way you're imagining," he said. "The way you've seen in movies."

"And I'm saying it might not have happened the way you think it would have either."

Gorpp didn't respond.

"Do you think the female delegate is attractive?"

He looked at her, then turned back to the window. "You already asked Overalls that question."

"And now I'm asking you."

"She is empirically attractive, yes."

Gabby got up then and went to the couch where she curled up against the pillows. Gorpp went over and sat with her, holding her. "I fail to see the relevance," he said. "I'm with you whether or not someone else is attractive."

"I don't know anything about your world, Gorpp, your culture. I don't know what to expect."

"Soon you will be able to form your own impressions, but you can be assured that none of that has anything to do with our marriage."

CHAPTER 18

GABBY HAD TAKEN to going into what they called The StarSail Coliseum, where Hank had set up the ring for Maxim and Gorpp's clash, where the first interstellar match, known to them anyway, had taken place. She'd begun using the room as a kind of sanctuary. There wasn't anything like a place of worship onboard and Gabby, while not particularly religious, needed a quiet place where she could sit with her thoughts. That's not what she found this time when she came into the StarSail Coliseum.

Instead she found Howie sitting with his legs crossed beneath him in the center of the ring. He had the lights trained on him, a white pool in a sea of darkness, the way Steve Levey would have had the spotlight on him back at the Bayfront Armory, as he set the stage for some of the most historic matches in the twentieth Earth century. The bright light made the puffs of white hair over his ears look like translucent electric charges going into his shiny bald head.

At first, Gabby thought maybe he was praying or meditating, but when he saw her emerge from the shadows he looked very alert, even intense, as he spoke to her.

"What do you really know of Enceladus?"

"Ha. That's the question, isn't it?"

"Did you know he was king of the giants?"

"I beg your pardon?"

"He's been written about through history. Oh yes, from Shakespeare to Keats to Melville. All of them and more have told the story of the great giant, Enceladus."

"Are you ok, Howie?"

"Never better," he said, looking more and more like a cult leader. "Like all the giants, he was born of the blood of the castration of Uranus."

"What?"

"Oh yes, by his own son. That's, well—"

"Howie, how are you adjusting to, you know, interstellar travel?"

"I have a great responsibility. I am the messenger, the scribe for a critical step in the history of our species."

"Well, that's some heady stuff. If you don't mind, I'm just going to sit in the back of the room for a while and have some quiet. I like to come in here to think."

"He was so big he used trees as spears."

"Ok."

"It's been said he is buried in Sicily? Even in death, the great giant causes the Earth to tremble and volcanoes to erupt."

"Wow, ok. Well, Howie, I'm going to go but I look forward to reading your story."

She left the StarSail Coliseum. It was clear Howie wouldn't be able to stop talking to her about the legends of Enceladus as long as she stayed, so she headed for the observatory and that cushy recliner she liked.

More and more, Gabby felt the creeping malaise return. She slipped into a deep sleep on the observation deck and when she woke next she wasn't sure how long she'd slept. Hours? Days? She'd started to wonder what time even meant but she couldn't concentrate for long enough to work it out before she drifted off again.

Days had indeed passed (by Earth measure) when she fully regained consciousness with enough focus to feel alert. At first, her mind couldn't reconcile what she was seeing outside the ship. It first struck her like fireworks coming from the surface of a planet, or moon, just off their starboard side. Her next thought was missiles being fired at them but there was something so intrinsically peaceful in the magnificence of this spectacle. Once her eyes, and her mind, came fully into focus, she realized it was the geysers of Enceladus that Gorpp had first told her about at the Maripole Hotel in Moscow, sitting before a fire on a snowy night in Mother Russia. There must have been hundreds of them, each shooting into the atmosphere. Those geysers, reaching for the stars from the gleaming ice of the surface of the moon filled Gabby with a feeling of peace she hadn't known since the day they'd spent with Ernie in The Conch Republic.

She wanted to be with her husband, to see this with him. She figured he would be on the bridge with Overalls and that's where she found him, along with the full delegation, newly departed from their self-imposed exile. When Gorpp saw her, he stepped away from his own kind and went to her. He put his hands on her shoulders.

"We have arrived at Enceladus," he said.

"It's so beautiful," Gabby said. She hugged him.

He hugged her back and whispered in her ear, "You're going to want to hold on."

"Attention," Overalls said into the intercom. "We are beginning our approach to Enceladus. Please hold on."

Then, the StarSail started its nose first descent to the ice-covered surface of the south pole of the moon.

"Are we speeding up?" Gabby asked over the din of the ship vibrating and rattling all around them.

"Very much," Gorpp said.

They both held onto a nearby bulkhead to keep from being swept off their feet and flung like debris across the deck of the bridge.

"Are we going to crash?"

"We have to build up enough speed to break through the ice on the surface."

"So, we're crashing on purpose?"

"The hull is designed to withstand the impact."

"Are you kidding me? The best your super advanced species could come up with is using your ship as a battering ram? That's not much different than Dimitri and Maxim's ice fishing methods, Gorpp. Or a piledriver in the ring."

"We do it this way because it works."

"Has it ever not worked?" Her words sounded like they were chopped into small pieces, like talking into a fan.

"There have been accidents."

"Has this ship ever successfully broken through the ice?"

"This is the maiden voyage of the StarSail 9000."

"Jesus Christ. We're all gonna die when we hit the ice, just like the *Titanic*."

"True, we are all going to die, but likely not as a result of breaking through the ice."

The tremors increased in frequency and intensity and Gabby lost her grip. Gorpp held on with one hand and grabbed a hold of her arm with the other, pulling her in close to an embrace. In her mind she saw her ballerina music box crashing to the floor. She tried to feel if Gorpp was scared. She couldn't tell. Things started to blur around her, as if she needed glasses. She looked at Gorpp, only inches away, but couldn't make out his features, then, a feeling like a beach ball skipping off your hand on its way to the next person, and things started to come back into focus. The tremors stopped. Outside, the viewscreen showed just blackness, no stars.

"Are we under water?" Her voice sounded clear, no more fan blades chopping up her words.

"Yes."

"And I never even felt the impact. Why not?"

"If the battering ram is of the right size and strength, traveling at the right speed, relative to the properties of, in this case a sheet of ice, it just slices right through with very little friction or resistance."

"So, what happens next?"

"Next, I show you the street I grew up on, the park I played in when I was young and where I went to high school."

"Smartass."

CHAPTER 19

THE HUMANS onboard seemed split about fifty-fifty between anxiety caused by what awaited them when they arrived on this alien world and the black nothingness surrounding them now, the feeling of inertness, going from hurtling through open space at previously unimaginable speeds to now pushing through the mass of a dark ocean pressing in on them more and more the deeper they went below the surface.

Gabby smiled when she entered the observatory. It was full of people for the first time. And there was nothing to see. The windows may as well have been blacked out. There was no light under the ice, deep in the ocean at the south pole of Enceladus. People seemed more intrigued with the inability to see out than they had with the wonders in plain sight along the way. Then they entered the immense underwater caverns that led to what had been home to Gorpp for most of his life.

People clamored even more to the windows and viewfinders in the observatory. Now, they could see it all. They were in a cavern alright. It was immense. And now the ship's lights were on, illuminating the rust-colored cavern walls. The cavern was so large, the StarSail traveled through it without coming anywhere near the edges that went out of the range of the ship's exterior lights.

Like a 747 taxiing at O'Hare or LAX, the slow glide through the cavern went on for a while, and then, with hardly a bump, the StarSail came to a stop. Gabby headed for the bridge to find out how the diplomacy was going to play out now that they'd arrived. When she entered, she saw a large panel had retracted and now opened into a passageway built into a dry part of the cavern itself. Gorpp and Overalls stood with the delegation from Central Command and watched as another delegation, from here on Enceladus, approached from the passageway.

Then, she heard the rumble of Maxim's Harley and smelled the acrid exhaust fumes and gasoline as he gunned the bike through the bridge and down the passageway, straight for Gorpp's people.

"Long live the Ring Raiders!" he yelled as he increased speed and left the Saturnarians leaping out of the way of this howling and growling apparition racing toward them. Gabby's brain was still so foggy she couldn't remember if this grand entrance was something she and Gorpp and Bobby had planned or if Maxim had just gone rogue. Once it happened, it seemed somehow familiar to her but she couldn't be sure if she was just remembering his arrival for the match with Gorpp or if it seemed familiar because they'd planned it. Or maybe just some kind of interstellar déjà vu. Either way, the rumble of Maxim's Harley had faded and he was gone.

As they got up and looked around, the delegation that had been nearly mown down reminded Gabby of how a cat reacts in embarrassment if it falls or misjudges a jump. It made her laugh. Which made Gorpp give her a look that reminded her of something else – her dad when he would scold her as a little girl for goofing off during a gymnastics lesson. The idea of Gorpp reminding her of her father made her laugh even harder. Which made him stare even harder. Before she knew it she was literally rolling on the deck, in tears she was laughing so hard. He came over to check on her.

"Are you alright?" Gorpp asked leaning down over her and helping her into a sitting position.

"Did you guys put laughing gas in the air down here?"

"This is the first time humans have experienced interstellar travel or the atmospheric conditions somewhere other than Earth or your own moon. The way you may react to certain --"

"The way you looked at me!" Gabby started giggling.

"Let's get you up."

"Let's get you up," Gabby mimicked, ushering in another gale of laughter.

"Is she alright?" White Eagle asked Gorpp.

"Yes. She may still be adjusting."

Gabby slid down the wall behind her and settled down a bit once she was back on the floor. She noticed the two Saturnarian delegations had mingled. It was clear, though non-verbal, that they were in intense discussion with each other. To her complete surprise, words, phrases, thoughts popped up in her mind like comic book dialogue boxes.

"stop the spread…"

"telepathic democracy…"

"already too late…"

"Rule Number One…"

"Gorpp…"

"already too late…" again and again.

Surprise turned to delight when she realized she was picking up the Saturnarians' telepathic transmissions, but it was quickly turning into a careful what you wish for situation as she started to feel like a small bucket being drowned with more information than there was room to store. The nausea came on so fast she was vomiting in violent expulsions of stomach acids before she knew what hit her.

Gorpp scooped her up and got her off the bridge, away

from the intense telepathic discussion taking place there. By the observation deck she was markedly improved. She looked up at Gorpp's stern face as he carried her and again, couldn't help but be reminded of her father. This time though, she just felt the protective concern they both shared for her and the comparison didn't seem so absurd. He set her down gently on a couch in the observation deck and sat close beside her.

"Well," Gabby said, "I don't know about the whole Maxim thing but that definitely wasn't the way I had planned to make my first introduction to your home world, that's for sure."

"A small part to a larger story yet to unfold," he said.

She rested her head on his shoulder and realized her ballerina music box wasn't the only familiar comfort she'd brought with her from Earth. "Thank you," she said.

CHAPTER 20

Gorpp, Overalls, Gabby, Bobby and White Eagle sat around the table in the room the delegation had holed up in for the last leg of their journey.

"The first order of business is Maxim," Bobby said.

Gabby noticed some gray creeping into his hair along his temples. Had that been there before they left? He had a gruffness about him that reminded her a little of Ernie. She was tempted to mimic him for being so serious, like she had Gorpp. "The first order of business..." She still felt like there was a trickle of laughing gas in the HVAC system onboard, like another fit of hysterics wasn't out of the question, but she held it together.

Over the course of the discussion, mostly between Bobby and Gorpp, it became clear they had discussed the idea for their first matches with Maxim but they'd never worked out the details or decided it was definitely a go. So there was that. Overalls said he would be in touch with their liaisons and keep tabs on him. A human on a Harley wouldn't be hard to find on Enceladus.

It also became clear, because of what Gorpp had described to her as telepathic democracy, that what they had hoped, and

Central Command had feared, had indeed come to pass. As word spread of the StarSail 9000's arrival, and who was on board, the telepathic information superhighway of Enceladus had been abuzz with curiosity, speculation and intrigue. There was no way they would be able to resist the supposed threat of being infected with Earthlings' primitive and violent tendencies if that meant turning the ship back and missing out on the big show.

They decided this group, along with a few others, like Hank, Coach Becker and Howie, would be the first to make an official visit, get the lay of the land as it were, and then decide on next steps.

Gabby had long lost track of so-called day and night since there was no daytime in space, or now, under a subsurface ocean. But after a rest, the StarSail delegation met on the bridge and departed down the corridor into the artificially constructed passageways deep in the underwater caverns of the moon's south pole.

"Will anyone from your world be meeting us?" she asked, a little nervous after her first encounter with them.

"No," Gorpp answered, but with no explanation.

She thought it odd and wanted to know why but she was also relieved. It made her try to remember Gorpp's people's version of the Earth expression, "don't look a gift horse in the mouth." Something like "don't ask why the ice didn't crack," she thought but decided not to ask. She gasped when the artificial passageway opened up into the raw rock walls of the underwater caverns.

"What's happening?" she asked.

"My people drained the water from a section of the caverns to use for living space long ago," Gorpp said.

"How big a section—" she started to ask but the enormity of the space they stepped into made the question obsolete. She imagined what the Grand Canyon must look like to a gnat but even that somehow seemed insufficient to give her the perspective needed to process her relative insignificance in the face of such an enormous space.

For some time, they all just stood and took it in.

"Guess I'm not gonna need my sunglasses," she heard White Eagle say, but she wasn't sure if he'd said it out aloud or just thought it. She didn't know if he would hear it, but she sent the thought back that it was plenty warm and he should be grateful for that.

"I feel like I'm inside an anthill," Bobby said. "Are all of those holes in the walls corridors?"

"Yes,"Gorpp said. "They lead to living quarters, working spaces, schools, everything. Above are all windows."

"And what is this space, this enormous space?"

"This is the center, where all the spokes connect."

"Like the town square," White Eagle said.

Hank set off walking toward the middle of the cavern. Gabby watched him get smaller and smaller as he went.

CHAPTER 21

Gabby was sobered by their expedition. No concerns about imminent fits of hysterics or even a giggle under her breath. She was spooked but on a scale she couldn't have imagined. They'd returned to their war room on the StarSail for a debrief.

"Tell me what you noticed," she said to all assembled.

"There were no advertisements. There was no art. No murals. No graffiti. Nothing. Once we entered into the main cavern, it all looked natural, the red rock surfaces looked untouched, even the openings to the corridors, none of it looked artificially created or even influenced, with the exceptions of the water being drained from the caverns, climate and air pressure controls being engineered and lighting," White Eagle observed

"If I visited Yankee Stadium would I be qualified to comment on Earth?" Gorpp asked.

"He makes a good point," White Eagle said.

"What about the fact that there were no people? I mean, it was a friggin' ghost town in there. I didn't see a single soul from the time we left the StarSail to the time we got back. Not a cockroach. Not a rat. Nothing. How is that possible?" Howie turned to Gorpp. "How is that possible?"

"They knew we were coming."

"They knew we were coming?"

"Yes. Of course. Telepathic news travels fast. They were watching."

"How?"

"Through windows. Through cameras. Through the minds of their neighbors and families. Our foray into the center place was witnessed by nearly every citizen of Enceladus. No one living on my world has met an extraterrestrial other than those like Overalls and me who were part of the occupation."

"How were the reviews?" Bobby asked.

"They are hungry for more."

"Asses in the stands," Bobby said.

"What does the government think?" Gabby asked.

"That word doesn't translate particularly well," Gorpp said.

"Don't give me that. You know what I mean."

"They didn't want us here."

"We know that. But we're here. Now what do they think."

"They're afraid. They see humans as a communicable disease whose influences and impacts could spread rapidly and wreak havoc."

"Do you think we're a disease?"

"It's complicated, but yes. In this context the analogy applies."

"That's lovely."

"Give him a break," White Eagle said. "You know he's right. Don't let your pride come between you."

"What?"

"Would you wish the seediness of Times Square or an oil crisis on these people? How about Viet Nam or Watergate?" White Eagle turned to Gorpp. "How many Saturnarians are incarcerated?"

"None to my knowledge," Gorpp said.

"How many murders last year? How many rapes? Kidnappings?"

"None."

White Eagle looked back to Gabby. "Cut him some slack," he said.

"What's the update on Maxim?" Gabby asked Gorpp.

Gorpp looked at Overalls.

"Where is he?" she asked.

"We don't know," Overalls said.

"What do you mean you don't know?"

"I've been in communication with our liaisons and they report that they are unable to locate him."

Gabby felt a nervous flutter of laughter that threatened to well up in her at the absurdity of it. "You're telling me your perfect, advanced society who all communicate simultaneously can't find a backfiring, stinking, belching motorcycle in their anthill?"

"I don't know what you people are talking about but I know what I need to do," Hank said as he made his way out of the room. Gabby hadn't even noticed him standing along the wall.

CHAPTER 22

IT WAS time for the two native Saturnarians, or Enceladians to be precise, to have their homecomings.

Even after the size of the first cavern they traveled through in the StarSail, and then the breathtaking Yankee Stadium of Enceladus, Gabby still had a preconception the passageways leading from the center space would be dark, cramped and claustrophobic, maybe with sconces on the walls and big spiderwebs in the corners. Quite the contrary.

Gorpp guided her through residential neighborhoods, commercial districts, campuses and parks. She hadn't allowed herself to really process where they were when Gorpp walked them up to the front door of a dwelling.

"Where are we?" She grabbed his hand before he could enter.

"You know where we are."

"Are you serious?"

"Yes."

"Why didn't you tell me? You never tell me things."

"You asked me to bring you to meet my parents as you had brought me to meet yours so that's what I've done."

"How do I look?" she said.

Gorpp smiled at her, for perhaps only the second or third time. "You are beautiful," he said. She smiled back. Then Gorpp's parents opened the door.

She saw both of their faces in his and felt the warmth she was accustomed to from him now enveloping her in a triangle of welcoming energy. She felt almost weepy and then a wave of resentment and exhaustion at her uncharacteristically emotional reactions to things lately. They crossed the threshold into Gorpp's childhood home without a word spoken aloud.

The physical and emotional experience Gabby had in Gorpp's parents' house was unlike anything, or even any combination of things, she'd experienced before. There was that odd feeling she could only compare to déjà vu, though that wasn't right. She had to admit, Gorpp was right, there were words, things, experiences that there just wasn't a precise reference much less translation for between Enceladian and English.

Walking through the spacious home, she sensed what it might be like to be a visitor literally walking through Gorpp's mind, his self. The walls in their home were more of the red rust colored stone. There were nooks and crannies. The floor wasn't all level. She saw what looked like a tree house or loft. Once they came to what her mother would have called the family room, she realized this home was designed similarly to the way the center space, like the spoke of a wagon wheel, with all the passageways leading off of it. She'd entered through one of the passageways so she didn't see it at first.

The family room was immense and rounded. There were really no right angles in the architecture or furniture. Everything had multiple dimensions and a vaguely New Mexico, adobe feel to it. About halfway up the wall the stone gave way to a convex clear glass that covered most of the ceiling. Outside the glass the ocean was lit by floodlights and, unlike when they'd entered through the cavern, the water teemed with life. Again, what Gabby saw seemed to try to retune her mind to adjust to this new reality. To give her a new frame of reference for what a jellyfish or a family home or a civilization can be.

"Let's sit," Gorpp said.

She heard it in her mind like the strum of a harp. And it sounded like such a wonderful suggestion. She could feel, in the background, his concern that she was overwhelmed by everything she was taking in, but in the foreground, it just sounded so wonderful, like fresh squeezed lemonade on a hot day. She noticed a vine crawling up the wall and wondered where it got light from, then complex schematics and diagrams flowed through her mind, but she couldn't process them.

Sinking into the couch she thought about how she'd imagined sitting with Gorpp's family, looking at old photo albums with black and white pictures and yellowing pages. Instead, she was treated to a mental kaleidoscope of home movies passing behind her eyes. She didn't understand all of it but she picked up on impressions, even smells and sounds, textures and emotions.

Then the sensation of moving in time. The filtered air smelled somehow brighter, the unseen but always just right lighting, was it a little crisper? The house looked different too. The stone walls and floors more textured, newer. She somehow understood she had moved back a generation, to be in the homes of Gorpp's parents, feel their minds, smell what they smelled, to feel the crossroads in their lives as a gravelly country road under the axis of her understanding. Sensory things felt somehow brighter but the boundaries of this place were smaller, confined by the limits of memory, even in advanced minds, compared with ours. By the time she traveled to Gorpp's grandparents' lives, it felt thin and bordering on claustrophobic, so much had been lost to time and translation and lack of attention through the generations.

It reminded her of the cedar trunk her mother kept at the foot of her bed, full of the remnants of her own mother's life: her diploma from the University of Georgia; a box of family pictures with the perforated edges, everyone always formal but smiling; letters; a box of wedding mementos; her collectible chinaware; a quilt she'd knitted. And one of the things in the cedar chest was an old cardboard shoebox containing one sepia tone wedding photo and a single infant-sized leather moccasin with beads woven into the sides. That was all that remained of her mother's mother. All there was to remember, to make sense of a life lived. A generation away from being all but forgotten.

Is that all we'll amount to, a shoebox with an old picture and a single baby's moccasin? There had to be more to life than that. She saw that whether it was a telepathic record among aliens on another world, or that old shoebox in her mother's chest, it amounted to the same thing.

Then, Gorpp's parents came into focus. She wasn't sure if they were sitting across from her or just appearing in her mind. She also wasn't sure anymore what the difference really was or what difference it made in the end. They were here. The two parts that had made the whole that was her husband. Their faces filled her vision. She could feel their pride in sharing Gorpp's childhood shifting to a need to hear from her about the Gorpp she knew. Not the functionary conscripted to the occupation ferrying cargo for Central Command. They wanted to know of this new Gorpp. Gorpp the Grappler. Gorpp the Champion. These are the stories, the images, the sounds and smells and textures they wanted now from her.

She leaned up from the cushions, trying to clear her head. Gorpp, sitting beside her, took her hand in his. That helped. She leaned back and opened up her mind and it felt like a vacuum, eagerly pulling out everything she could show them. She saw the slide show as they did. Gorpp showing up in the parking lot after her match at the Charlotte Coliseum. In street clothes no less. Earth clothes. Going back to her apartment. Gorpp tapping his foot to the rhythm of a Tom Petty song. She was vaguely aware of them accessing other parts of her mind to learn enough about Tom Petty to give the situation some context. She could feel them looking intently at the things they passed on their drive that she hadn't even consciously noticed. Street lights. Signs for fast food joints. A homeless person sitting in front of a cheap motel.

They saw the first time she seconded him in the ring. A blur of his greatest matches. The ones she'd seen anyway. She saw their trip to Alaska. She could feel their interest in Gorpp's interactions with Overalls. They were there for the wedding. At first, she felt embarrassed as their consciousness found its way on their honeymoon. But after just a few moments of apprehension, she felt a wave of calm. It became akin in her mind to worrying about God seeing you go to the bathroom or change into your swimsuit.

By the time they'd gotten to The Conch Republic, the assembling of their cast and crew for this trip, Steve Levey's heart attack and Maxim's dramatic entrance on the StarSail, she was having trouble keeping up with their mining of her memories, her consciousness. Gabby was vaguely aware of Gorpp gently cautioning them about being patient as they rummaged in her box of memories. They tempered their curiosity and made sure to treat this new and strange creature their son loved with care as they explored the garden of her mind with delighted fascination.

Gabby remembered Gorpp's mother putting a wonderful covering over her, cool to the skin but warm inside. It smelled like Christmas vacation to Gabby and the fabric seemed to intuit where to snug her in close and where to let her move and breathe. She slept better on that couch than she had during the entire voyage on the StarSail.

When she woke up she almost thought she smelled the salt air from the Gulf the night she'd run away from home when she was seventeen. She noticed the floors were the same uneven red stone but polished smooth. She wondered if that was done on purpose or was the result of a long life of walking on them.

She felt like she should need to pee when she woke up from what was certainly a long sleep. But, like on the ship, she didn't. Convenient though it was not to have to worry about eating or eliminating, it took some getting used to. She then thought she smelled coffee but she'd never smelled coffee that smelled that good. She let her nose guide her and found Gorpp's father in what she supposed could be compared with our kitchens and dining rooms. He was manipulating a nozzle attached to a steaming beaker. It reminded her of an old b-movie about a mad scientist but it smelled like a cross between a humidor and coffee beans roasting, maybe with a touch of cinnamon or chicory. She pulled her covering around her so her chin snuggled into it as she entered the Gorpp family kitchen and laboratory.

"Good morning," she said.

Gorpp's father looked up at her then adjusted a dial on his apparatus.

"It smells delicious."

"Gorpp thought you would appreciate it."

"This was his idea?" Gabby smiled. "Well, he was right."

He went back to tinkering.

"Why don't you have any art?" she asked, looking around at the bare stone walls. "Or family pictures?"

He regarded her. "Don't we?" He pointed to his temple and she got a rush of the images they'd shared last night, from Gorpp's childhood to their journey from Earth.

"Ok, ok," she said, motioning for him to turn it off, which he did. "You made your point. I guess it's just an adjustment."

"Just as Gorpp has had to adjust to live in your world."

"Touché."

He served her the coffee-like drink in a metallic cup that

felt cool to the touch on the outside. She took her first sip on an alien world.

"It's delicious. Can I get some to take back to a friend?"

"Gorpp told us your friend Ernie would want us to pack some for you."

Gabby took another sip. "Do you find it odd that your people can't find our missing crewmate?"

"I find it implausible."

"You don't think Overalls would lie, do you?"

"Just as you're experiencing some challenges assimilating the necessary information to process what is happening here, he had his own challenges on Earth. I knew him when he left. I don't now."

"You do think he's lying."

Gorpp's father didn't deny it.

Gorpp and his mother came in then from what looked like a solarium. They each had plants, berries and flowers in their hands. The way Gorpp's mom looked at him made her think she must have picked up on subtle mannerisms or body language from Gabby's mother when she met her in Gabby's mind. She immediately felt her presence as familiar, comforting.

Gabby felt the echoes of a conversation between Gorpp and his parents. She felt her own thoughts fully exposed.

She took another sip, then thought, "what if I need the bathroom?"

"We have accommodations," came the reply.

"That's embarrassing," Gabby thought.

"Irrelevant," came the response.

Then she smelled fresh baking Nestle Tollhouse chocolate chip cookies, saw the countertop in her own parents' kitchen, in her mind. The smell and image had a syrupy falseness to them. They were trying to distract her from feeling embarrassed but did it in a sloppy way. The memory for which they had no independent context, felt too thin when constructed for Gabby. Then she tuned in to what Gorpp and his parents were talking about. He'd picked up on his father insinuating he didn't believe Overalls when he reported they couldn't find Maxim.

She got a little woozy as she concentrated more intently on their discussion. Gorpp guided her to a kind of hammock chair that snuggled into her form the way the blanket had and made her feel secure. She lost a little time in the hammock chair but came to feeling refreshed. And apparently Gorpp's family's version of coffee didn't have the unfortunate laxative effects of our own.

When they stood at the door saying their goodbyes Gabby and both of Gorpp's parents got emotional. She could feel a flood of appreciation coming from them for sharing all she did about Gorpp's great accomplishments in her world, but more than that, for loving him, taking care of him, standing up for him when they no longer could, for taking that responsibility, looking out for their cherished son.

As they walked down the front walkway, Gabby said, "those cookies your mom made smelled a little funny at first, but they were so good!"

CHAPTER 23

Overalls' homecoming was very different. Even as he approached his house, he could tell something was off. Did the stone need washing? Did the lighting array need adjustment? Had he just been away so long he'd forgotten? No, something wasn't right. He went in to find even more darkness and shadows. The silence felt stale, not a pause but a full stop. He walked through the corridors of his home, looking for an answer to explain what had happened. The vines here, unlike the ones at Gorpp's family's home, lay dead and brittle on the floor. The only smell, that of uncirculated air, unlived life.

He'd known, of course. The Dear John letter was a universal phenomenon. She'd grown weary of his absence and his status quo reports. Instead of being intrigued by his entrance into the wrestling business, she'd been embarrassed, first at the notion of her soldier off on Earth, slumming. Then, worse, he couldn't even do that right. She sent the letter then. He responded but that had been when he stopped getting messages back from her. When she severed their neural link.

He was foolish to allow himself to believe when Gorpp

presented the unexpected opportunity to return home, that it wasn't already too late. He paced around the house, covering ground he'd already surveyed. Looking for things missing, things left behind. Any signs. Any messages, explicit or symbolic. Desperate for some last drop of connection to squeeze out of a connection that had dried up.

He stood in the center space, a gray, dismal and most of all empty cavern. He thought back to his unilateral decision to leave Steve Levey behind. He'd justified it to himself as a romantic, even heroic gesture. Now, standing in the shadows of his former life, it felt petulant, selfish, and downright delusional. And all too human.

He'd been standing in the same room with him but didn't even notice him, hunched there in the corner. And Maxim didn't acknowledge his host. Of course, in his analytical mind, Overalls knew she was gone or he wouldn't have sent Maxim to his house to hide out. He'd modulated his sensor array to scramble Maxim's life signs, temperature and even atmospheric displacement. He would be invisible other than to the naked eye. And he'd taken similar measures to ensure his thoughts about Maxim wouldn't be detectable. Maxim wasn't crazy about stashing his bike on the way but he couldn't very well have just parked it in front of Overalls' pad.

"Are you altogether well?" Overalls asked him.

"Do I look altogether well?"

Aha, Overalls thought. A classic example of a rhetorical question. Overalls caught on to how those work quicker than Gorpp. He didn't answer.

"Did they pick up my bike?"

"No."

"They've gotta know where it is."

"Oh yes, we all know where it is."

"So, why would they just leave it there?"

"Why would they pick it up, as you say?"

"Well, I'm going to get it."

"And take it where?"

Maxim stopped. There was nowhere to take it.

CHAPTER 24

Maxim started to wonder what he was even doing here. He'd had a lot of time on the voyage from Earth to Enceladus to think about the day Earl Kruddup, Jr. had shown up at the White Walrus Pub. Maxim had been drinking alone in the middle of the day. He was one of the few people there. When the door swung open the big triangle of light blinded him. He couldn't make out who had walked in until the man was standing right in front of him.

"I thought you were in prison," Maxim said.

"I got out."

Maxim looked around the mostly empty hole in the wall bar. "What are you doing here?"

"I came to see you," Kruddup said.

Maxim smirked. No one ever came to see him. It seemed absurd on its face. He took another sip of his beer and turned away from Kruddup, as if he wasn't there.

"I came a long way to see you, son. You want to hear me out."

That last was a statement, not a question. Maxim kept staring straight ahead, studying the bottles lined up behind the bar. He took another sip of his beer.

"The people who sent me here are problem solvers with deep pockets. They want to help you with your problem with the Henchmen and line your pockets too. How about that?"

"The mafia wouldn't take you and neither would the Syndicate." Maxim gave the bent and balding Kruddup a disapproving once over. "The feds don't hire felons and you don't ride, so I'm just trying to figure out, who sent you?

"I do represent the Syndicate," Kruddup said, saddling up to the stool next to Maxim. He raised a finger at the bartender, pointed at Maxim's mostly empty bottle and put up two fingers. Then he pulled his wallet out, put a business card on the bar and slid it in front of Maxim who read it without picking it up.

Earl Kruddup, Jr.
Special Projects
United Syndicate of Professional Wrestling

Maxim slid the card back to him, finished his beer in a gulp and pushed the empty bottle away. "Anybody can print up a business card to say anything they want. I could go get one that said I was the president. But it wouldn't make it true. I don't have anything to talk to you about," Maxim said, then he counted out some cash, put it on the counter and walked out.

When Kruddup emerged into bright light of day, Maxim was waiting, leaning on his bike. Kruddup paused, then walked slowly toward him with his awkward gait.

"It doesn't add up," Maxim said. "Why would the Syndicate hire you?"

"I gave you my card," Kruddup said. "Special projects."

Maxim shook his head. "It doesn't add up," he said again. "They don't need you." He looked at Kruddup like he was a shit stain.

"Don't you get it?" Kruddup said. "Special projects. Dirty

work. The shit they don't want to do. The jobs where you get your hands dirty."

"That's what you took your long trip for?" Maxim said. "Dirty work? You came to my backyard to do dirty work?"

"Who are you? Prince Charming? You afraid to get a little dirty?"

Maxim looked down. He didn't like talking. He didn't like Kruddup. And he didn't like anyone interrupting him when he was drinking.

"Son, you've got a real problem with these Henchmen." Kruddup said, leaning in close, like somehow, in this empty gravel lot, someone was going to hear him. "They mean to put you and your uncle at the bottom of a very cold lake if you don't get right with them."

"What would you know about them?"

"I know they've got enough dynamite to blow a hole in Mount McKinley big enough to ride that motorcycle through."

Maxim had heard enough. "Go home, Mr. Kruddup." He cranked up the sputtering and belching old engine on his Harley and sped off in a spray of gravel and gas fumes.

CHAPTER 25

Earl Kruddup Sr. hadn't liked his son, Earl Junior, or his wife very much. And no one, it seemed, like Senior. Bitter way to grow up. Junior had never seen any path other than treachery. Maybe if he had been taken away at birth and placed in a good family he would have turned out different. But that didn't happen.

A snake oil trial lawyer named Danny Fireside got Junior a reduced sentence and he was out on the streets. His father's house, his wrestling territory, his livelihood, were all gone. He had nothing left but scores to settle. He stood outside in that gravel lot, cold, hungry and far from selling Maxim on his plan. But he did think it was a good sign that he'd waited for him. If he really wasn't interested, why wait?

It had taken four flight changes, nearly twelve hours and more than four thousand miles to get from Mobile, Alabama to Alaska's Kenai Peninsula. More importantly, the cost of the trip had left him with just the cash in his pocket. No more big fancy Cadillac. No more pimply-faced kid to drive him around.

Kruddup didn't entertain notions of a rise back to glory. He was resigned to his misery. He just wanted to bring as much of that misery to his enemies, his betrayers, as he could. He had his wits and a bitter determination. It was Gorpp he hated most. Gorpp was the mastermind, the one who'd stolen the world title from Heavyweight Championship Wrestling of the Southeast and used it to get rich and famous while Kruddup ate mealy grits in a white collar federal detention center.

He knew he mustn't underestimate Gorpp as an adversary. Lord knows, many had made that same mistake with *him*. He decided he couldn't come straight at him. That's when he heard, through what access he still had to the wrestling grapevine, that Dimitri was done, a hobbled shadow of his former self.

One of the most feared wrestlers of his time. All those years in the ring had made it unnecessary to hurt him physically. He decided instead to take the one thing he had left. His family. His sanctuary. His home.

Dimitri never would have imagined Kruddup showing up here. He may have had his problems with the local MC, but the thought of Earl Kruddup Jr. in Homer never crossed his mind. But here he was, worming his way into Maxim's head. He would use the Drozdov boy as a pawn to bring down Dimitri and Gorpp at the same time.

The alien freak backstabbed him with Buddy Graham and then his high-flying bride broke Kruddup's ribs.

Of course, Maxim was right that the Syndicate wouldn't have hired him in a million years. He was a felon, a pariah. Blackballed. A desperate free agent, hellbent on destruction.

CHAPTER 26

GABBY STOOD with her back to Gorpp in their quarters. She had her hands on her ballerina music box but she didn't open it. Gorpp sat behind her looking out at the cavern wall outside the ship, just as he did at the passing stars. She turned and went to him, put her hands on his shoulders. He didn't respond at first, then he reached his right hand across his chest and rested it over her left.

"Why are you sad?"

Had he said it out loud? It didn't matter. He'd said it.

"I'm still thinking about everything your parents shared with me. I've always seen you as larger than life. To see how small you were here, among your own people. It hurt my feelings. I'm trying not to be resentful toward them for not seeing how special you are."

He squeezed her hand and she felt the thought enter her mind that soon his people would see Gorpp the Grappler, Gorpp the champion. He wasn't actually the champion on Earth anymore but he was on Enceladus.

"I want to show you something," he said with another squeeze of her hand. He stood and led her out of their quarters. They went to the bridge and then through to the corridor that led to the center place of Enceladus. Gabby hadn't seen it since their first time leaving the ship. Her last memory was of an immense red rock cavern with countless openings leading to passageways, windows, neighborhoods, communities and a culture that still remained a mystery to her. She remembered Hank walking off into the vast openness of the cavern, a man with a mission.

This time, as they entered the center space, it was a coliseum on a level Gabby couldn't have imagined. Being from Georgia, she'd been to Sanford Stadium in Athens. She thought the capacity there was ninety-five thousand. This was a sea of faces until all she could see was a blur like the ripple on the surface of a lake. She even saw faces in the irregularly-shaped windows along the walls of the cavern.

Gorpp guided her forward, into the crowd. Again, like gentle water, like one organism, they parted and created a path for Gorpp and Gabby. They walked like that for a long time it seemed, through the gentle sway of his people.

"They're so quiet," she thought. But Gorpp heard her.

"They're in spirited conversation."

"Why is it so quiet then, for me? I can hear you now sometimes. And your parents certainly came through loud and clear."

"It's too much," he said. "It's so loud you can't hear it. I can only hear bits and pieces as we move through them. Like overhearing a conversation at a restaurant."

"What are they saying? What are they talking about? Why are they all here?"

"They're feeling energized, awakened. We're what you would call the talk of the town."

"This is about us?" She felt so small in this sea of what felt like every Enceladian. And that's when she saw it.

There was Hank, standing in the corner of a fully constructed ring, tightening a turnbuckle. He appeared nonplussed, almost unaware of the sea of alien beings engulfing him. And it wasn't just the ring. He'd been busy since Gabby paid a visit to the in-laws. He had the announcer's desk with the ring bell and microphones. He had the lights set up and shining down into the ring. There weren't enough folding metal chairs on Earth for a crowd this size. They'd brought enough seats for the first few rows but beyond that it was standing room only in the Enceladus Coliseum.

They reached the ring apron and Gorpp escorted Gabby up the aluminum steps and through the ropes and into the ring. The crowd that didn't say a word also didn't applaud when the stars entered center ring, but Gabby felt a press of intense interest, like psychic applause. It made her brain tingle with a kind of satisfaction that was so intense it bordered on uncomfortable. Like hearing the echo of the conversations that would overload her primitive human circuits.

Hank gave them a quick wave then hurriedly continued his feverish preparations.

"Why are they here already?"

"The ring," Gorpp said, motioning around them.

"This is just the stage," she said. "We haven't even announced the show."

"Nothing much new happens around here very often. First contact and a show, that's not going to take much effort in the way of advertising or publicity."

"What do they think is going to happen?"

"The conjecture is broad ranging and hotly debated, but none of it is anywhere close to what we'll actually do."

"They're so smart, but they're also like children playing with the wrapper instead of the present."

Gorpp gave her a look.

"They can hear me, can't they?"

"The ones nearby, they'll pass it along to the rest, so yes."

"Don't you ever want some privacy?"

"I'm accustomed to it."

Gabby looked around at the rapt faces of the crowd. "This is going to be the biggest wrestling card in history," she said. "We need to get with Bobby and work out all the final arrangements. Like, where's Maxim, for starters."

CHAPTER 27

SITTING around the table in the meeting room on the StarSail were Gorpp, Gabby, Bobby, Overalls and White Eagle. The time had come to take the broad strokes of their plan for the most historic wrestling event of all time, and fine tune them into a run of show.

This was still in the territory days, the old school days of kayfabe, when it was the cardinal sin to even hint, much less admit, that professional wrestling wasn't a true competition with unknown outcomes. A time before the Syndicate monopolized the business and brought the whole thing under one roof. And a time when the good ones could still adlib a promo and call a match in the ring with just some basic instructions: watch out for the other guy's bad right knee, take it about fifteen minutes, make him look good for the hometown crowd then finish with the piledriver. Stuff like that.

"What's our first order of business?" White Eagle said.

"Before we get into it, I just want to let you know, Howie asked me if he could attend this meeting, as a member of the press," Bobby said.

"What did you tell him?" White Eagle asked.

"I told him he was crazy for even asking and that I better not catch wind he wrote one word about the fact that there even was such a meeting. That's what I told him."

"I've talked to him," Gabby said. "This trip has had a big impact on him. He's not the same. He's not looking at this through the lens of *World Wrestling Digest*, or kayfabe, or any of that anymore. He sees himself as a messenger, a witness to history, which he is," she looked around the room. "We all are. He believes he has a higher calling than to report on this as a wrestling event. He sees himself more as Carl Bernstein or Mike Wallace than Howie Shows."

"Then what does he care about sitting in this room then?" Bobby said. "Cause all we're gonna talk about is wrestling."

White Eagle raised an eyebrow.

"Anyway," Bobby said, "I just wanted to let you know he asked. I told him no. Let's get down to business. The angle is, Earth is here to counterstrike against Enceladus because of their attack on our planet. They declared war. We're here to answer the call. Our narrative is that Gorpp took over Earth and when Maxim defeats him, we will have won back our planet and taken over theirs. Gorpp assures me, while this will sound like utter nonsense to them, because it is, that it will still be irresistibly intriguing and we'll have them on the edge of their seats, so to speak."

"Let's start at the start," White Eagle said.

Gabby looked at Overalls. "Are you ready to be our Steve Levey?"

"There is no need for an announcer here," he said. "My people—"

"You're missing the point," she said. "The announcer's job isn't really about the announcing. For the most part, fans know who the wrestlers are or they don't care. The announcer is there to set the stage. To tell a story. A good announcer can make all the difference."

"I will set the stage," he said.

Gabby looked at Gorpp but he had his usual poker face.

"Let's move on," Bobby said.

Gabby felt sick to her stomach about Overalls' ability and understanding of the importance of doing justice to announcing. It turns out she needn't have worried.

CHAPTER 28

When Gabby saw Overalls backstage in white wingtip shoes, black checkered slacks, a Hawaiian shirt and a wine-colored and wide-collared sport jacket, she almost cried. The only thing he was missing was the cigar. He stood in the corner, subtly jogging in place, muttering to himself. Clearly deep in concentration. But when Gorpp looked at him he might as well have called his name.

"I'm ready," Overalls said.

No one spoke or whistled or yelled out a drunken "woo hoo!" in the leadup to the matches, but there was a hum of energy in the room that felt like a pressing, electric weight to the Earthlings.

Hank flipped a switch and spotlights flooded the ring. White Eagle had placed every spare hand he could in different spots throughout the crowd. As soon as Hank lit up the ring they all started clapping and hooting and hollering, real rowdy. Then Gorpp sent the thought out, like a virus multiplying throughout the crowd, that what these humans were doing was the correct etiquette in this situation. He appealed to their sense of diplomacy in urging them to join in clapping and, yes, hollering. It only took a few adolescent Enceladians to get others going and by the time Overalls was climbing up onto the ring apron, the cavern was filled, for the first time in eons, with a roaring crowd.

Suddenly, the entire cavern went dark, except for the spot on Overalls in the center of the ring in all his 1970s Earth and Steve Levey glory. Hank looked at Gorpp in the shadows backstage and Gorpp nodded at him. He'd dimmed the house lights in some way that didn't involve mechanical levers. The crowd quieted, leaving only an echo of their outburst. Gabby had a vision of the real Steve Levey, who dreamed of going to the stars, on his back in a hospital bed at Tampa General. Could he still be there? It seemed like a veil covered her life on Earth.

The mic lowered down and Overalls reached up for it, cleared his throat and said with a commanding voice that filled the cavern like a rush of water, "Laaaaaaadies and Gentlemen, welcome to history in the making as two worlds collide. It's Earth versus Enceladus and the fate of both worlds hangs in the balance!"

What looked like spotlights danced over the crowd, adding to the mood of anticipation and trepidation in the center place. Howie Shows sat at a folding table at ringside, scribbling furiously in his pad. There was no local press in attendance, or in existence for that matter, having been rendered obsolete by a species with such advanced telepathic abilities.

Wade "Big Wave" Rich and Heavyweight Championship Wrestling's Florida champion, Willie Winston, wanted to wrestle as a tag team called the Florida Flyers, but Gabby, AKA the "highflying Firefly," said they had to change it, so they went with the Florida Fantastics. They took on Dallas

"Lightning" Jackson and "The Ugandan Giant" Makusa. Makusa made it clear to Gorpp and Gabby he wouldn't be pinned anywhere in the solar system either by what he regarded as a pretty boy in Rich, or a flamed out college football player in Winston. So, Winston won the match for the Fantastics with a spectacular dropkick that stopped "Lightning" Jackson in his tracks.

Of course, Enceladians weren't aware of the rivalry between Gabby (Firefly) and Coach Becker but they seemed to feel it in the air, in the energy between the two women.

As in their past confrontations, Becker worked to keep Firefly from climbing up on the ring ropes to launch her aerial attacks. The older, stronger woman's advantage was in keeping Firefly grounded where Becker's superior amateur mat skills would keep her in control. And her strategy seemed to be working as Firefly appeared more and more frustrated after being caught first in an armlock, then a half nelson, and then a leglock.

As if they'd heard her crying for help, "The Puerto Rican Princes" Mia Camilla and Katie Camaro burst from the backstage dressing room, still half in their street clothes, and attacked Becker from behind, raining blows on her back, neck and head until she relinquished the leglock on Firefly and lay prone on the canvas.

But Firefly wasn't in league with Camilla and Camaro. She didn't fight dirty and she didn't need help from outside the ring. As the ref yelled at the attackers to stop, Firefly appeared to be recovering from the leglock and realizing what was happening. In another twist, she climbed to her feet and then to the top turnbuckle where she launched her signature cross body block, perfectly timed and positioned to take out both attackers who ran from the ring as soon as they realized Firefly was up and after them.

Firefly tended to Coach Becker but she was apparently unable to continue.

After supposedly conferring with Bobby at ringside, the referee seemed to be explaining to Overalls what the final outcome of the match would be under the circumstances. Overalls stepped into the ring, the mic lowered, and he explained to the crowd that Becker would have been ruled the winner by disqualification but the fact that Firefly rescued her from her attackers showed she wasn't complicit in the attack, so the match would be recorded as a draw.

Howie frantically wrote it all down, then swapped his pen and pad for a Canon 35mm camera with a telephoto lens and got a shot of Overalls from the white wingtips up to the collar of his Hawaiian shirt overlayed against the burgundy of his sportscoat.

Firefly helped Becker back to the dressing rooms and White Eagle's plants cued the crowd that polite applause was appropriate to recognize Becker's recovery and Firefly's sportsmanship.

Most people don't know that the first time Ozzy Osbourne's "Crazy Train" was used at a sporting event was on Enceladus. It was the Earth-year 1982, in the main event match between hometown hero, Gorpp the Grappler, and the betrayer, Maxim Drozdov. It wasn't part of the plan mapped out by Gorpp, Gabby, Bobby, Overalls and White Eagle. The truth is, if Maxim had been on board with their plan, he would have entered the ring first, to Judas Priest's "Hell Bent for Leather." As it turned out, after some delay waiting to see if Maxim would show up, Gorpp decided to go with Plan B. He went out first, with his trademark ring walk song, "Flyin' Saucers Rock & Roll."

Of course, no one on Enceladus had ever heard the song. Most had never heard any music at all, at least not in the narrow way we define it. Some Enceladians would tell you they hear the universe, the pulse of their civilization, the collected knowledge and insights of an advanced collective. A repetitive and simplistic rockabilly song would be a vulgar and unwelcome assault on their basest of senses.

Hank put a mic up to the portable Panasonic cassette deck he'd brought from Tampa and ran it through the main PA system and the twang and cymbals of Billy Riley's Little Green Men filled the cavern. The rinky dink PA wasn't anywhere near big enough for this seemingly endless cavern in the center space of Enceladus, but to the locals it was an almost unbearable cacophony, at least at first.

At first it was an assault on the senses. Enceladians didn't communicate verbally at all. They didn't play instruments. They didn't have concerts. They didn't really make any noises for the sake of making noise. Not only was the PA insufficient but with no risers, most of the many thousands of Enceladians at the matches couldn't see what was happening in the ring. But that didn't matter either.

Like a sophisticated and telepathic game of telephone, those who could see and those who could hear relayed the information back to those behind them like a mental baton that was then passed all the way around the crowd. But unlike telephone, the last in line got a very real visual and auditory replay of what those in the front had seen and heard with their own eyes and ears. The time delay was perceptible to them but wouldn't have been to us.

The way Plan B worked was they had Gorpp go out first, as bait, to see if they could lure Maxim from the shadows. They didn't know what he wanted, what his motive or end game was, so they sent Gorpp out and figured if Maxim didn't show, they'd have Machete Marquez take his place.

Marquez had shown little respect to Iron Claw Martinez, who had come out of retirement for the umpteenth time for the match. Old Iron Claw had started out in Lucha Libre in Mexico City, then moved on to the US southwest and worked his way up to being a headliner. He'd toured the Caribbean,

Canada, Japan and even down under, in Australia, through a decades long and storied career, but, like most guys, he hadn't been smart about the money, and what the hell, he'd never been halfway across the solar system either, so he took his licks from the stiff and mercenary masked man, Machete Marquez.

Gabby couldn't hear the thoughts of the giant throng of Enceladians and she couldn't gage how many were male and how many female, but she picked up on that same sense of heat when Marquez wrestled as she did at Madison Square Garden, and then she regretted that Gorpp would know she'd thought it. Turns out advanced species hadn't evolved beyond jealousy.

It wasn't ideal bringing Marquez out again after having wrestled on the undercard, but they figured the home crowd wouldn't really care who Gorpp dispatched of to save them from Earth's invasion, as long as the hero won. And he'd been sufficiently savage against Iron Claw to make him a credible adversary for Gorpp.

Gorpp brought up all the house lights and there he stood, behind the curtain, preparing to make his ring walk and be seen, for the first time by his people, as Gorpp the Grappler, the hero, the defender of their world. The simple black curtain parted and those who could see him took in this vision of Gorpp in a flowing white silk robe with a big feathered collar, and enough sparkling rhinestones to have made Elvis, Liberace and Gorgeous George proud, and **TRUE CHAMPION** across the back. It was the robe he'd worn in the double-cross match in Mobile when he'd taken the world title back from Dimitri. And as in that match, Firefly, in all her finery, accompanied him to the ring, this time not just as his second, but as his wife.

They slowly made their way down the aisle to the ring and fawning Enceladians, young and old, gawked, took mental pictures and sent the images around the cavern. Gorpp and Gabby nodded and slow walked their approach to maximize the moment, to add to the buildup for the match, and, to give Maxim the maximum amount of time to show himself. It reminded Gabby of the footage of Ronald Reagan making his entry onto the floor of the House of Representatives for his first annual State of the Union address. Eventually, they made it to the ring and Gorpp climbed through the ropes parted by Gabby and Overalls. When he waved to the crowd, there was no prompt required by Bobby's plants in the audience. The place erupted in cheers, applause and whistles for their home world boy made good.

Gorpp hadn't shared it with Gabby, but this moment was made all the more prescient for his people because they'd learned of Gorpp's having been afflicted with Poison Ocean Syndrome on Earth and, in their time, was facing his imminent demise. They were aware too of his acceptance of having sealed his own fate since his vaccine was in the shipment he failed to deliver when he abandoned his post to set out on a quest to singlehandedly take over the Earth. They knew too that he had accepted his fate to live out his few remaining days by the side of his Earth bride, the glamorous and acrobatic Firefly. It was telepathic tabloid journalism and they ate it up just like we do the *Star Globe* and *Enquirer*.

Even as he walked around the ring, waving to his people, Gorpp lowered the house lights and left just Hank's ring lights on. He didn't see but felt his parents in the crowd, their pride was felt by those around them and quickly spread throughout the cavern, the latest wrinkle in the story of a hometown hero. Overalls stepped to the center of the ring and Hank lowered the mic down.

"Ladies and gentlemen, please allow me a point of personal privilege as I introduce, not just the greatest heavyweight champion in the history of professional wrestling, but also Saturn's son, the incomparable conqueror of worlds and defender of Enceladus, Gorpp! The! Graaaappler!"

The fevered applause was deafening to the ears and the mind as an entire civilization greeted their savior, not just from some supposed overthrow by these primitive Earthlings, but from the tedium and monotony of a society without entertainment, without scandal or intrigue.

Flattered and humbled as he was by this reception from a world who hadn't noticed him leave and, had it not been for what he'd done on Earth, would never have noticed if he didn't return, he couldn't help but scour the crowd for any signs of Maxim. He hadn't been able to see Maxim arrive backstage and give his own cassette tape to Hank. Machete Marquez would have to settle for his conquest of Iron Claw Martinez after all. Maxim nodded to Hank and he pushed play on "Crazy Train." As Randy Rhoads' iconic guitar riff echoed through the cavern, Gorpp brought the lights back up just in time for his countrymen to hear the Son of Blackbird crank up the engine of his old Harley backstage and then see him burst through the curtain at such speed it seemed inevitable he would crash into the ring, if not the crowd.

At the last possible moment, he skidded to a stop just at the apron and leapt from the bike into the ring. He wore black boots and trunks along with a Voss matt-black half helmet, John Lennon-style shades and his cut, a black leather jacket but with new rockers, or patches, on the back. Where before it had read "Kenai Henchmen" along the top and "Alaska" at the bottom, his jacket now read "Ring Raiders" on the top and "Saturn" on the bottom. He stomped around the ring, eliciting genuine fear from those in the first few rows that then rippled through the crowd like a contagion. He ripped off his sunglasses and helmet and threw them down. Then, instead of taking off his cut and going to his corner for Overalls to introduce him, he grabbed the mic from him and looked out at the crowd.

He raised the mic to his mouth, then grimaced and put it back down. He looked at Gorpp who responded with his typical deadpan expression, giving nothing away. He didn't know Maxim, didn't know why he'd fled and, for the most part, had only seen him behave erratically when in his presence. Maxim squinted at him, Gorpp couldn't say for certain if he picked up on regret or even some feeling of apology, but then, whatever breeze of second guessing had blown across Maxim's mind, was gone. What remained was the steely resolve of the betrayer, the suicide bomber who feels inseparable from a destiny of destruction and indistinct from those in its path. Standing between Gorpp and Gabby in all their finery on one side, and the almost comically colorful Overalls as Steve Levey on the other, he raised the microphone to his lips, and this time he spoke. His voice carried far and his words carried across all of Enceladus.

"Look around you," he said. "What do you think you're seeing? This is a joke." He almost spat the words as he shot a glare at Gorpp. He walked right up to the edge of the ring directly in front of Howie Shows, made eye contact with him, then said directly to him as he wrote, "Wrestling. Is. Fake." He looked around at the crowd. "This is all a show. The circus is in town and these are the conmen on the midway." He gave it a minute to sink in. He'd crashed the biggest event in wrestling history to commit the cardinal sin, an unforgiveable betrayal.

No one moved. No one spoke.

"This," Maxim said, pointing at Gorpp, "is no champion. And I? I am no threat to you. I am just a messenger. Here to pull the curtain back on a fraud before it spreads to your world." He looked again at Gorpp, then dropped the mic on the ring mat, got out of the ring, cranked up that smelly, noisy old Harley and cleared a path of startled Enceladians before him as he carved his own way out of the cavern, leaving Gorpp, Gabby and Overalls standing in the ring.

White Eagle had the presence of mind to cue Bobby's plants to start applauding, and it worked. The crowd who were judging the entire experience on a sustained degree of intrigue, and not on kayfabe or any knowledge of the traditions of Earth, wrestling or these particular wrestlers and their relationships, found the entire performance to have kept them at a peak of intense engagement.

Their applause, as it had been for Gorpp, was sincere if not spontaneous. Maxim was long gone into one of the caverns' many passageways and didn't hear it. Gorpp, Gabby and Overalls quickly followed White Eagle's cue, stepping to the center of the ring, joining hands and bowing like it was Shakespeare. After several bows eliciting waves of renewed applause, Gorpp opened up his robe, revealing his old world title belt. Gabby and Overalls helped him out of his robe. Gorpp wore his old plain military uniform he'd always wrestled in, an eggshell white body suit with matching belt and boots. He reached behind him in a familiar motion, unclasped the belt and thrust it up over his head with both hands. Howie snapped the shot for the cover of the *Digest* and the applause reached a decibel level never before recorded on Enceladus.

CHAPTER 29

Bobby summoned Howie to the meeting room on the StarSail like a kid to the principal's office even though Howie was twice his age, and all too eager to come, pad in hand.

"Sit down, Howie." Bobby gestured to a chair on his right. Howie sat, flipped his pad open past all the pages filled with his small, tightly packed blocks of text, looked at Bobby, uncapped his pen and waited.

"You can't write it," Bobby said.

"It's written." Then he wrote down what Bobby said.

"And you can't write about this meeting either. It's off the record."

Howie wrote that down too.

"Are you listening to me?"

"Intently."

"What the matter with you, Howie?"

"Nothing that I'm aware of. A little arthritis, but at my age I can't complain."

"You're gonna put yourself out of business if you shit on the business. You know that."

"I don't think so."

"No? You think people are gonna keep coming to matches, keep buying magazines about a bunch of made up stories?"

"Yes."

"That's a big gamble."

"I don't care."

"Look," Bobby raised his voice. "Cut out the fucking Carl Bernstein crap, Howie." Bobby looked down at the floor, took a deep breath and composed himself before he looked back up at Howie. "I can't let you write this."

"Are you threatening me?" Howie asked with delight, then furiously scribbled down Bobby's statement.

Bobby leaned in close, like they were secret coconspirators. "Look," he said, "we invited you on this trip with a certain understanding."

Howie wrote that down. "And what was that understanding?" Again, that almost devilish grin.

"Jesus Christ. Really? Getting screwed over by Dimitri's cousin, I can live with that, you know? But you, Howie? We go back."

Howie got it all down.

In another flash of anger, Bobby snatched the pad away then just threw it against the door and spoke without raising his voice. "Get out," he said.

Howie picked up the pad, noted down that last bit and took his leave, muttering under his breath in excited tones. What a scoop.

CHAPTER 30

THE ORIGINAL PLAN had been to have these inaugural matches as a way to kick off the Earth counterattack angle and then tease it out over a series of cards on Enceladus and maybe even other colonies and outposts. Thanks to Maxim, and now Howie, that all seemed to be in question. But maybe it was more than that. Maybe it was more that they'd all failed to anticipate just how much their arrival, their spectacle would captivate Enceladus.

Gorpp told Gabby he would meet with the Enceladians to gage just where they stood on the prospect of future cards. What he learned was that in record speed, for his people, they had moved on past the Earth storyline and started to stage their own version of post-kayfabe era wrestling theater all across the caverns of their society, acting out different Shakespearian melodramas complete with cross body blocks, figure-four leglocks and sleeper holds, not to mention lavishly adorned characters that started with influences from Gorpp's almost Gorgeous George-like robe to Firefly's bright color schemes to Overalls' Steve Levey impersonation. But, the fashion-component of this new craze, like the storyline, had evolved in countless ways at a rapid pace and was now far beyond any of those things and more like its own kind of art trend.

It was just what Central Command had feared, what they'd tried in vain to stop. Humans. Before they spread. Gorpp decided it was high time for them to clear out and head back to Earth. He sent a signal to Overalls. They met in the center of the now mostly empty cavern. There was no litter of popcorn boxes and beer bottles left behind like there would have been if this had been on Earth. Hank was dismantling the ring at Gorpp's behest. Overalls wore the white wingtips with lime green slacks, a white leather belt and a silk checkered shirt.

"What is this?"

"A Tribute," Overalls said.

Gorpp rolled his mind's eye at the clumsy lie.

"I'm staying," Overalls said, almost petulantly. "My services are needed here. I'm the announcer extraordinaire of Enceladus. I've found my niche here at home, as you did on Earth."

"Very well," Gorpp said. "We're going now."

"Prudent," Overalls said.

"May the ice never crack on your path," Gorpp said.

"Or yours."

And they parted ways.

Gorpp said goodbye to his parents alone. He was concerned about what the heightened emotions would do to Gabby.

He asked their liaison from the delegation how the governing body viewed their responsibility vis-à-vis Maxim rumbling through the caverns on his primitive, polluting and obnoxiously loud Harley lowrider. The terse response he got was that Maxim didn't even make the list of their top concerns right now given the epidemic of Enceladian-style wrestling that had interrupted energy production, greenhouse crop harvesting, academic research and core functions of government.

It was likened to a strong narcotic-strength addiction plaguing upwards of ninety-percent of the population. Numbers the likes of Ernie Cantrell or Sam Calvin could only have dreamed of. But with so many proverbial asses in the stands, it was not only changing their culture in garish and vulgar ways, according to some, but was indisputably causing major disruptions across every sector of their society.

Gorpp shared the news that Overalls would be staying only with their inner circle but somehow Howie had it almost immediately. He was asking for an interview with Gorpp about it. Gorpp had no interest.

Gorpp wondered if there would be any move to stop them from leaving in the StarSail but none came. He wasn't surprised. They were preoccupied with the professional wrestling plague he and Gabby had unleashed on Enceladus and they were probably still contemplating how to respond to something as infrequent as theft among their own kind. Not to mention, leaving is exactly what they wanted them to do.

Bobby called a meeting in the room where they'd staged their in-flight fight night to fill everyone in on the plan to return sooner than anticipated.

"So, you're saying we came all these millions of miles for one match?" Machete Marquez said.

"Billions," Gorpp answered. "It's billions of miles, not millions."

Howie sat cross-legged on the floor, writing it all down, snapping pictures of the animated exchanges.

"You can choose to see it any way you want," White Eagle said.

"Yeah, chief? How do you see it?" Marquez said with a sneer.

"That we had a once in a lifetime opportunity to be

ambassadors to another world and made history to boot." He decided to ignore the racial slur. And he didn't point out he hadn't even gotten to wrestle at all. Some said he was over the hill, but if they said it to his face he was known to challenge them to find a hill and see who could climb to the top faster. One newbie training with the Syndicate, hoping to get a spot, was fool enough to take him up on it. White Eagle climbed to the top, then met up with the winded and chastened young wrestler, catching his breath about halfway back on his way down.

"That's how I see it," Hank said from the back. He didn't mention to anyone he still had Maxim's *Blizzard of Ozz* cassette. Funny, it came from Earth but it was his favorite souvenir from the trip. When the Son of Blackbird burst through that curtain on his howling Harley Davidson to the strains of "Crazy Train" he could feel the hair on his neck and back tingle.

"I'm homesick anyway," Katie Camaro said. A few nodded.

"I'm sure ready to get some sun and hit the waves," Wade Rich said, doing a kind of impression of surfing, though the truth was there weren't many real waves in the Gulf unless a storm was brewing.

Gorpp had engaged the auto-pilot before the meeting started so as they spoke the StarSail unmoored from her dockings, glided smoothly through the watery caverns and then started her ascent, gathering speed to break through the surface ice, then rise up into the rings and eventually make her way to Earth.

CHAPTER 31

As soon as Howie felt the very subtle lurch of the StarSail leaving its moorings on its world of origin, he started feeling itchy. He scratched at his arms and his neck, up under his stubbly chin and even on the top of his shiny, bald head. And then he started to feel like there was something in his eye. He rubbed at his closed right eye with the back of his hand with more and more vigor. He tried flushing it with water. He couldn't see anything in there, but it felt like a hair lodged between his lower eyelid and his cornea. And was that his arthritis he was feeling in his writing hand?

He sat on the floor in a corridor somewhere in the bowels of the StarSail, cross-legged with his back hunched as he wrote furiously in his pad. When he got to the end of the page, he realized his vision was blurred. He couldn't even read what he'd written. And he couldn't remember either. He felt like his thoughts, his memories hadn't just reflected, but dumped out of his head onto the page he couldn't even read. When he let go of the pen his hand stayed locked into place, still grasping at a pen that now lay on the floor. With some effort he was able to pull his fingers apart. He winced and broke a light sweat as he clenched his hand into a fist, then relaxed it back out.

After a few deep breaths with his hands turned palm up and his eyes closed, he reached both hands up and scratched at the base of the tufts of hair poking out on either side of his head. His scalp itched like hair lice making snowmen with thick drifts of dandruff. But he couldn't find either when he looked in the mirror. In spite of the pain in his cramped and arthritic hand, and having lost his train of thought entirely, he still felt an urge, a need to scribe. He'd been validated on an interstellar stage. The universe didn't pick Ed Bradley or Mort Castle to document this historic first for humanity. If he needed to ice his hand and get some help to format the issue of *World Wrestling Digest* that would make him a household name, so be it. He was here to document history in the making. The mechanics of reporting it was work he could outsource if he had to.

"There you are," Hank said.

Howie looked up and Hank came right into focus.

"You ok, Howie?"

Howie looked at Hank like he were an exotic squid in an aquarium.

"Bobby wants to see you," Hank said.

That seemed to snap Howie out of his trance. "Summoned to the principal's office again?" Howie said.

"He just said he needed to see you."

"Right away?"

"Seemed like."

Howie started climbing to his feet, slowly. His joints creaking as he did. "I don't see what the big rush is. We just left. Won't be back for what is it anyway, weeks, months?" he grumbled. "Bobby isn't Captain Kirk up here, you know? He's just Ernie Cantrell's old enforcer."

"I think he just wanted to talk to you," Hank said.

Howie scratched at his bicep until big red welts raised on

the skin. His winking right eye gave Hank the creeps. He lurched off down the corridor.

Howie flung the meeting room door open and found Bobby alone at the head of the table. Howie sat at the opposite end, flipped his pad open and waited.

Bobby rubbed his eyes. Howie noticed they were red. "Can we skip the pad this time? This isn't about me giving you information. It's about me asking for it."

Howie thought for a second, flipped the pad closed and put his pen on the table.

"Thank you," Bobby said. He ran both hands through his hair. "Look, Ernie always operated under the principle that you look out for your guys. You didn't have to like them. You didn't have to socialize with them. But if they worked for you, you had to pay them and you had to have their backs. No exceptions. But, you know, he didn't suffer fools or turncoats either." Bobby looked down at the table, then back up at Howie. "Maxim betrayed not just us, he turned on our whole business. But I also left him behind on that crazy planet, or moon, or whatever. I'm struggling here, Howie."

Howie listened but didn't have a response.

"Something I learned even before I got into wrestling, when I was boxing in the service, you have to understand your opponent, his motivations, his weaknesses, his habits and history. I don't know much about this kid. I know he's Dimitri's nephew. I know he had a bad accident and after that Gorpp sent Dimitri sailing into that group of sick kids when they wrestled, it set something off in Dimitri. I know Dimitri taught Maxim, the ringwork, the psychology, the business. I know the kid got in over his head with some one-percenters up there in Alaska. But I can't make any of it add up to what he did, you know?"

This was no Captain Kirk sitting before Howie, alright. He put the pad back in his pocket and the pen behind his ear. He steepled his hands and put his elbows on the table. "There are some things I can tell you. Some I know. Some I think I know."

Bobby leaned in.

Howie looked back at the closed door then started talking. "He kept to himself during the trip. I hardly saw him except for the match he had with Gorpp for the Enceladian delegation. The few times I saw him from a distance he was brooding, didn't give the impression I'd get a warm reception if I asked for an interview."

Bobby listened intently.

"But then, right before the matches on Enceladus, he appeared out of the shadows in the center space when I was looking for good places to get a wide angle shot or two. He motioned for me to follow him into one of the caverns and quickly led me to a dark corner, out of the way."

Bobby imagined Howie thinking he was meeting with Deepthroat in a DC parking garage.

"He didn't tell me what he was gonna do but he did say he was a spy sent by the Syndicate."

"What?"

"That's what he said."

"And you didn't tell us?"

"I actually tried."

"You told me you didn't have time to talk? You remember?"

Bobby looked away. He remembered.

"He told me nothing would ever be the same after the main event."

"He was right about that," Bobby said, still looking at the wall.

"I'm sorry, Bobby."

For a time, both men sat in silence in the small meeting room, not looking at each other. Then, Bobby seemed like he's processed what Howie said and was ready to move forward. He met Howie's gaze.

"You said you were going to tell me something you knew and something you thought you knew. What do you think you know?"

"That he was lying," Howie said.

"You think he was bullshitting you about being a spy for the Syndicate?"

"Yes, I do."

"What makes you think that?"

"Well, for starters, did he think he could betray you, all of us, that way and then still hitch a ride back to Earth?"

"Apparently not," Bobby said.

"So, what was in it for him then? The story would make more sense if the Syndicate offered to put him on the big stage but they can't do that if he's riding his old Harley around under the oceans of Enceladus, can they?"

"That's a good point. So what's the truth you think you know?"

"I think he set the whole thing up, the Kenai Henchmen threat, the Syndicate story, all of it."

"But why?"

"Because he hates Gorpp. He blames him for what he sees as strongarming the title away from his uncle. For stealing his thunder and his glory. His family's legacy."

"But Gorpp and Dimitri are good as far as I know."

"That may be but Maxim is fiercely loyal to Dimitri. I don't think he cares if Dimitri is ok with it. He isn't."

"You think the whole thing, from the motorcycle gang threatening him to the Syndicate story is all bullshit."

"I don't know for sure about all the pieces and parts but I believe he's acting on his own behalf and those are his motivations. Did you notice he couldn't even look at any of us? Like a criminal who doesn't want to humanize his victims for fear his conscience might get in the way. And the fact that he clearly knew from the start he couldn't come back seems to support my theory."

Bobby turned it all around, looking at this new information, and unsubstantiated theories from every angle.

"Bobby, you didn't leave him behind. He never intended to come back to Earth. Ernie would be proud of you."

It was the last coherent conversation any of them were to have for some weeks.

CHAPTER 32

GORPP PILOTED, navigated and maintained the ship as he moved around through sleepwalkers and space zombies. The Eye of Jupiter was upon them. The zombies filled the observation deck, White Eagle, Howie and Gabby among them. Like lemmings, they flocked to the big windows onto the solar system, now filled with the bloodred Eye of Jupiter, the mother of all storms.

Howie scribbled furiously on his pad as if he were watching a morality play or a court case, not a faraway and centuries old storm. Jupiter came on them much quicker on the return and the Earthlings' neural functions, bodily rhythms and metabolisms were adjusting all over again to high speed space travel. Gorpp didn't feel threatened when he saw White Eagle hold Gabby's hand as they teared up together lost in the swirling torrents of the red eye. Gorpp noticed the writing on Howie's pad as he passed close by him. It wasn't English. At a glance he couldn't discern any pattern in the markings on his pad. He stepped up behind Gabby and put his hands on her shoulders. She melted back into him. They didn't need to speak for him to comfort her.

Howie flipped the page of his pad and wrote as fast as his trembling hand would allow.

Gorpp got Gabby settled in to her favorite chair on the observation deck with a blanket from their quarters. He would check on her again after he made his rounds. Along the way, he found Hank trying to assemble the ring again. He had all the parts spread out in geometric patterns across the floor. He sat in the middle, muttering to himself, holding a turnbuckle in one hand and a wrench in the other, turning this way and that. He seemed a little agitated but Gorpp thought he would work through it so he continued on. He knew Bobby and Howie were in the meeting room, he assumed so talk about kayfabe and leaving without Maxim.

He came across a card game with Katie Camaro, Coach Becker, Machete Marquez, Willie Winston, and Winston's aunt sitting around a table drinking beer and a couple of them with cigars. Depending on who was dealing, their card play resembled everything from poker to rummy to card tricks. He could sense no internal consistencies but the players all seemed to be intuitively in synch with each other.

Gorpp performed routine maintenance as indicated by his diagnostic analyses of the ship's systems. He did his kind of cross between meditation and yoga. He checked on Gabby. She was lucid for the first time since they'd gotten up to speed on the return. But confused.

"Where are we going exactly?" She looked around their sleeping quarters a little panicked.

"Home," Gorpp said, sitting beside her.

She looked around, at the stars outside their window, passing at incredible speeds. "I know, I mean, I know we're going home, but, I'm sorry. I'm, for some reason I'm having trouble remembering some things. Gorpp, I'm scared."

He brought her in close, wrapped her in his arms. "It's alright," he said. "It's not surprising. I should have told you, your brains may decide it's too much to process and decide not to make the memories entirely accessible, at least at first."

Gabby hugged him back but didn't really know what he was talking about. She remembered Steve had a heart attack. She thought maybe she'd had a dream about meeting Gorpp's parents. And she had a feeling something happened to Maxim, but she couldn't remember. She looked at the stars passing outside the window just like they did on long car trips as a kid.

Bobby spent a lot of time in the ship's gym. It took him a while to get the hang of the nautilus-like equipment, but it turned out to be pretty intuitive, even for a space zombie. Gorpp sat on a stool as Bobby finished a kind of hydraulic bench press and sat up, wiping sweat from his face with a towel pretty much like our towels.

"Is your mind clear yet?" Gorpp asked.

"Clear enough, I suppose. Something on your mind?"

"We haven't worked out the story for the return."

"True," Bobby said. "I guess I am still a bit fuzzy on all that. I'm still sorting out if we're coming or going. Then I'll figure out to where."

"I'll check back with you," Gorpp said, and left the gym.

As he walked the corridors he reflected on Maxim's plan succeeding but failing to have any of the meaning he'd intended. It reminded Gorpp of when he realized the world champion of wrestling wasn't actually the world champion of Earth.

He found Gabby asleep on the observation deck. He didn't want to disturb her but he knew she wouldn't want to miss the Red Planet, so he gently stroked her bangs and whispered her awake in time to see the planet as they passed.

"From Down Under to the Dark Continent," was the headline White Eagle came up with and Howie just ran with it from there. As people awakened and became more clearheaded, no one really talked about what they remembered, or didn't, about where they'd been, how they'd gotten there or what they would say when they returned. But tall tales of their adventures Down Under and on the Dark Continent felt like an emotional sav of comfort to their brains, overloaded with trying to process space travel, contact with an alien race and all the rest. Gorpp provided the angles for the matches, similar to the ones they used on Enceladus. Howie accepted them enthusiastically, as if subconsciously he knew it was true. Howie's article would say Maxim stayed in the Outback and joined an OG motorcycle club called The Bushrangers.

Gorpp brought them in hot to the parking lot at the Bayfront Armory to add another spell of disorientation at the end of the trip in the hopes it would make discounting anything to do with space travel or alien contact more palatable for their subconscious, and conscious minds. Once he had a parking lot full of space zombies he started muttering about jetlag and the long flight from Melbourne.

Gorpp had to remotely activate the ethereal elevator so he could return the StarSail to the occupation hangar above them. In just a few moments for us, he navigated the StarSail from the Bayfront Armory in Tampa to the hangar it came from far above the Earth inside the Enceladians' occupation force. As he expected, he received no communication as he made his approach, had no security checkpoints and no problem gliding the ship right into the hangar and back into its slip.

Gorpp surveyed each deck, each quarters and each passageway, inspecting them for wear or stain or need of any attention. He'd already gone through the ship thoroughly, cleaning and tinkering and taking account. He found Gabby's ballerina music box and put it with his things. The humans hadn't been clear-headed when they returned. That was for sure.

He entered the station and as he walked through the

passageways he could feel he was no longer anonymous. He started to pick up on mental communications. He walked into the mess and stood in the middle of the crowded tables and a flood of information came into his mind. He saw Hank's ring, surrounded by onlookers on Enceladus, he saw the matches and Maxim's betrayal, then a blur of the wrestling fad, or plague, depending who you asked, that swept across their home world. But he also saw that like a brush fire, it had spread quickly, burned bright and already mostly been extinguished by its own superficiality.

Gorpp put the question out asking what had come of Overalls in his guise as the Steve Levey of Enceladus. The images that came back to him were surprising. He saw Overalls, having traded in his burgundy sport coat and white wing tips for a black leather jacket, helmet and goggles as he rode beside Maxim through the back caverns, belching exhaust from two Harleys, or one Harley and a spot-on replica. They were the founding members of the Ring Raiders MC. It sounded like things were largely back to normal with this one conspicuous exception of having an outlaw motorcycle club rumbling through their bowels.

Gorpp was asked if he wanted to stay, if he would stay?

He declined and made his way back to the StarSail and his small transport tucked away inside.

CHAPTER 33

He touched down on top of the Ambassador Hotel, next door to the Armory and walked over to the parking lot at the Bayfront. He found Gabby trying to calm down a frantic Howie Shows. Gorpp stepped up his pace and came on the scene.

Howie paced and pulled at his hair, knocking his pen out from behind his ear. "It doesn't make sense," he said.

"It's his notebooks," she said to Gorpp. "He can't make sense of them."

"Well, can you?" He whipped one out of his shirt pocket and flung it open, revealing page after page of bizarre shapes and interlocking patterns, doodles and equations, but no reporting in any recognizable language about anything that had transpired since last they stood in this parking lot. "They're all like that. I filled up dozens of notebooks on this trip and they're all shapes and equations and nonsense. But it's not just that. Why can't I remember what happened? I can't even remember the flight from Melbourne. How is that possible? "

Gabby looked at Gorpp. She saw his parents' faces and

had lots of echoes of impressions of things just out of reach. A cavern. A giant red eye.

"All I've got is White Eagle's 'Down Under to the Dark Continent' angle. That's stuck in my brain like glue. And it's sure not because it's an original idea. Oh, and Maxim staying behind to join up with some Aussie motorcycle gang."

"Do you need a lift to the airport?" Gabby asked him.

"What I need is a bonfire for a big pile of notebooks filled with gibberish. You got one of those?" Howie wandered off for a bit.

"I left my music box," Gabby said to Gorpp.

"I have it," he said.

"You do?

"Yes."

"That's wonderful. You're wonderful." She hugged him. He hugged her back. She looked up at him.

"Seriously though," she said, with a quick glance at Howie zigzagging around them, muttering to himself. "What happened? And why can't we remember, or even write it down? That's creepy."

"Some of it may come back over time, but I'm not surprised."

"Did you know this was going to happen? What happened to us?"

Gorpp looked around, surveying who was still in the lot and who had already left.

"Are you listening to me? Did you know?"

"I suspected," he said.

"I feel like we've already had this conversation," Gabby said.

"We have."

CHAPTER 34

STEVE LEVEY never checked out of Tampa General. He'd spent much of the time only semi-lucid. The doctors told Gorpp and Gabby he talked with the nurses and other staff a lot about going into the sky, into space. One of the nurses started to wonder if he had been an astronaut he talked about it so much. He'd passed away a few days before their return but they made it in time for his memorial at the Columbia Restaurant. It was a who's who of wrestling's biggest names, the likes of which hadn't been seen since Gorpp and Gabby's wedding at the Don Cesar, just over the Sunshine Skyway bridge, in St. Pete.

John White Eagle greeted them at the door as the press snapped pictures of the Florida, national and even international wrestling luminaries who had come to Ybor City to pay their respects. Steve Levey was no tough guy. He'd never stepped foot in a ring without a microphone in his hand. But he was a larger than life figure in Tampa, in Florida and in wrestling the world over. Everyone there, including the ones lining the street for a block in each direction outside, were there because this was Steve Levey.

The wait staff carefully guided the mourners to their seats.

Sam Calvin and Ernie Cantrell had known Levey the longest and they found themselves sitting side by side in the front row. Gabby sat on Ernie's other side with her parents, Dr. and Mrs. Miller from Buckhead in Atlanta. Bobby was beside her, then Nat Pfeifer and White Eagle. Howie Shows could have had a spot in that front row but he didn't think he'd be able to sit still. He had remained in an agitated and confused state since their return. How could he not remember any of it, even the flight back from Melbourne? How come all his notes were gibberish? It didn't make sense. The loss of his old friend, and such a foundational pillar of wrestling as he knew it, only added to his anxiousness. Better to be milling around the crowd, looking for places to snap a picture, staying on the move. He'd crawl out of his skin trying to sit still.

Bobby motioned for Hank and his wife and sons, who were standing along the wall in the back of the restaurant, to come up and take their place as respected members of their fraternity. Earl Kruddup, Jr. knew better than to show his face in Florida but his old assistant, Carol, who hated Junior's guts, came to pay her respects. Every member of the StarSail's compliment that made the trip to Enceladus was in attendance. They didn't really remember what had happened to them, or couldn't process it, couldn't assimilate it consciously. Half of them had convinced themselves they really did wrestle in Australia and in Africa. It was mostly a crutch, something to lean on to try to make sense of a void filled with confusing emotions and thoughts but little information or recall. But they had all shared an experience. The not knowing was a shared experience as much as whatever it was they couldn't recall.

Gorpp was doing his version of meditating, or just tuning out the here and now to move through time more efficiently, when the minister called his name, it turned out for the second time. He stood from his chair at the end of the front row and went to the podium that had, until this afternoon, been the hostess stand. Gabby had insisted he wear a suit. There hadn't been time to get it fitted, but the standard sleeve length forty-eight regular in coal black with newly shined black dress shoes conveyed the champ's respect for their fallen comrade. Gorpp had been thinking about the cigars he'd smoked in Key West, or the Conch Republic. About how too many of those cigars were what had robbed Steve Levey of his dream to go to the stars. He reached the lectern, gripped the sides and raised his almond-shaped eyes to survey the packed room. Most of the faces were familiar.

"Good afternoon," Gorpp said.

"Good afternoon," came back a low murmur from those assembled.

"We are here today to pay our respects to Mr. Steve Levey, known for decades as the voice of Florida wrestling, heard around the world. If you look around this room, here in his —" Gorp paused, looking at Gabby. "—his beloved hometown of Tampa, you can see that people came from around the world to make it known the value the wrestling community placed on Steve Levey.

"Gabby and I spoke with the physicians who attended him at Tampa General. They had come to interpret Mr. Levey's constant talk of traveling to the stars as a way of him reckoning with his own death by imagining an ascension into heaven as what awaited him. Apparently, it's not uncommon. But that's not the truth. My way of honoring the life and legacy of Steve Levey is to tell you that truth.

"Ladies and gentlemen, as I've made no secret of since my arrival here, I'm not from your world. I come from under the oceans of one of Saturn's moons that you call Enceladus. Earlier this year, my wife and I decided to take wrestling to my world. Our first stop was to talk to our mentor, Mr. Ernie Cantrell."

Gorpp gestured to Ernie in the front row. Ernie

remembered well Gorpp and Gabby's visit and their plan to take wrestling into the stars. He wondered if it was kayfabe that he hadn't heard word one about that trip, just Howie's *World Wrestling Digest* version about Maxim's "dirty tricks Down Under."

"We then recruited the best in the business." He stopped to look at Bobby and White Eagle. "I stole a spaceship, picked everyone up at the Bayfront Armory and off we went to the rings of Saturn."

He heard how ridiculous it sounded. He noticed people whispering to each other. Were they wondering if he'd lost his faculties? He forged on.

"I want you to know, we invited him to make that boyhood dream to go to the stars a reality. He came very close. We very much wanted him to come. He knew what we were planning and he couldn't wait to set off on an interstellar adventure." Gorpp's gaze drifted up.

"And the one you know as my evil twin carried the Steve Levey torch, doing his best to replicate his wardrobe, his style and his contribution to professional wrestling. And he played a central role in having wrestling catch on in a feverish way on Enceladus."

Gabby massaged her temple gently then, after a disapproving glance from her mother, put her hand back in her lap. Gorpp wrapped it up. As he made his way past the priest and back to his seat, Gorpp saw Howie sitting cross-legged in aisle, weeping, trying to write it all down.

Later, White Eagle would ask Howie why he never ran it in the *Digest*. Howie told him it was because it sounded too ridiculous, even for *World Wrestling Digest*. But they both knew, on some level, in some universe, it was true. It wasn't the kind of thing you ever got used to.

John White Eagle never did go back to freezing his Florida balls off in New York. The next time Gorpp and Gabby saw him he was back wrestling alligators in the Everglades, joking around with tourists and signing autographs. He'd put on a few pounds. He said he'd never been happier.

At one point during their visit, White Eagle had one of those lightbulb moments.

"I'm gonna get a boat," he said. "And I'm gonna name it the *ROS Dissonance*."

Gabby looked at Gorpp but he didn't look back.

"Where did that come from?" she asked.

"I don't know really," White Eagle said. "It almost felt like a kind of déjà vu. You know, the kind we've all been having since the trip. I mean, all of us but him." He pointed at Gorpp.

"Honestly, the name came to me before the idea to get a boat." He looked a little flustered.

"Why ROS?"

"Oh, you know, like Royal Mail Ship. RMS."

"So, why ROS?" Gabby asked, not at any of it made much sense, except that it did.

"Royal Outer Space," he said. "Like I said, from what I hear I think we've all been having some strange thoughts since the, well, the journey we took."

Machete Marquez did return to the Syndicate where he was welcomed back thanks to the gates he drew for the moneychangers in the front office. Willie Winston still wrestled, on the independent circuit in Florida, more as a hobby. But he got hired on at Waverly Furniture to do promos for them in Tallahassee where he was still a local legend from his days making a run at the Heisman at Doak Campbell Stadium.

After the whupping he'd taken from Machete Marquez, Iron Claw Martinez convalesced on the trip back to Earth and, once again, announced his retirement as soon as they got back. It became a footnote in the *Digest* story about the tour of the Dark Continent and the land Down Under. Wade Rich went back to Sarasota and launched a new line of "Big Wave" branded surfboards, a nice side racket to supplement his wrestling income that just wasn't the same as the pre-Syndicate days. Marquez got "The Puerto Rican Princes" Mia Camilla a shot at the USPW in a dual role as his valet and wrestling women's matches.

After all the press about Heavyweight Championship Wrestling's tour of Africa, there started to be real demand for "The Ugandan Giant," Makusa, to actually wrestle in Uganda. The Republic of Uganda was in the thick of a guerilla war that would result in Yoweri Kaguta Museveni taking power in 1986. "Lightning" Jackson started managing Makusa after their return from Enceladus and though they decided it wasn't safe to actually wrestle in Uganda in 1982, word had spread throughout Africa about the Ugandan Giant and Jackson was able to book him to wrestle in safer places on the African continent. Some of their cards nearly rivaled the sixty thousand in attendance in Zaire for the Ali-Foreman "Rumble in the Jungle" in 1974.

Hank got that picture he'd hoped for at the start of the journey, not just with Gabby but with Gorpp too. Howie took it and Overalls had developed it somehow that Howie couldn't begin to understand. And Gorpp and Gabby both signed it for him. A rare wrestling collectible, if not one of a kind.

The rigors of interstellar travel on the brain function of this crew of Earthlings, and especially Howie Shows, protected kayfabe from Maxim's betrayal but it wouldn't be too much longer before the Syndicate betrayed kayfabe themselves.

Gorpp and Gabby decided they owed Dimitri a visit and they found him ice fishing, as if he hadn't moved since their first time finding him here, but alone this time. He looked a little better but they weren't crazy about the idea of him out there by himself if something happened. Gorpp relayed the story he'd told at Steve Levey's memorial. He told him of Maxim's betrayal that ended up evaporating in the memory banks of the humans onboard. And he told him about the Son of Blackbird rumbling off into the caverns under the freezing oceans of Enceladus. Dimitri didn't have much to say beyond remarking that he missed having his nephew around to help him with his fishing gear. Gabby wasn't sure Dimitri was altogether there. He seemed muted. Dulled.

"Why don't you come with us to Key West?" Gabby said. "We could have you in the sunshine faster than you could change into your swim trunks."

"In your spaceship."

"Yes, in our spaceship."

Dimitri never responded.

For a while, Gorpp and Gabby sat patiently with him in silence, and just waited. Gabby would later tell Gorpp she thought she saw a tear in the Russian's eye when she put a hand on his shoulder before they left. He never did respond.

Their next stop was Timbuktu. Gabby thought it would make her father smile to get that postcard from her with a Timbuktu postmark. Gorpp didn't get it but that was alright. They were followed up the dusty road by a group of Tuareg children wearing what looked like sheets, some with colorful patterns, others plain. After figuring out how to mail a postcard from Timbuktu to Buckhead in Atlanta, the United States, they were followed by the curious and friendly children back to Gorpp's vessel where they watched in awe as Gorpp and Gabby boarded, closed the airlock and ascended into the heavens.

Gorp's ship was so fast over small distances – like anywhere on Earth – it almost got to feel like teleportation. So, Gabby realized within a few moments when they hadn't arrived in Key West.

"What's wrong?" she asked her husband.

"Nothing. I wanted to take a moment to ask you a question."

Outside the window, the aerial view of the Kenai

Peninsula quickly changed to the vastness of space, stars and galaxies. He'd tried to explain it to her but Gabby still didn't understand where the energy came from to power his ship.

"So, ask your question." Gabby never had any idea what Gorpp may say next. It was part of the fun of their relationship.

"How did you know Overalls was going to replace Steve Levey?"

"What? What do you mean?"

"Back in your 1979, at the Don Cesaar, when you first brought up the idea of taking wrestling to Enceladus, you said Overalls could be our Steve Levey. How did you know that?"

"I, I don't know. I mean, I don't know that I did know that."

"You said it."

"I believe you but they're not the same thing."

"How could you have known to say it if you didn't know it would be true?"

"Honey, I think you're reading into something that isn't there."

"I understand," Gopp said, they touched the controls and they were making their descent onto the thin strip of sand in the Florida Gulf still officially called Key West.

"What do you think you understand?" Gabby said.

Gorpp brought them down for a landing behind their friend Duck's place then turned and regarded his wife.

"I understand it is possible to know things you don't realize you know."

"Your brain exhausts me sometimes," she said.

Gorpp didn't respond to that.

"There's one thing I still don't understand," Gabby said. "Why did Overalls do it? Why did he conspire with Maxim?"

"I asked him that," Gorpp said.

"Yeah? What did he say?"

"Boredom."

"Boredom?"

"Yes, boredom with the monotony of his life in the occupation. He jumped at the chance to be part of a secret plot with Maxim for the same reason he was so eager to make the voyage home."

"I don't get it," Gabby said.

"Really? It made a lot of sense to me."

They took Duck up on his offer of blended daiquiris and a Gulf view but Gorpp took a pass on the cigar. They knew their old mentor, Ernie, would have some questions for them. The Conch Republic's secession had failed almost as soon it began when they surrendered to a nearby Naval officer. Prime Minister Wardlow was back to plain old Mayor Wardlow. But the worldwide attention his little stunt garnered resulted in the feds removing the checkpoint after all and the tourism dollars rolled in.

EPILOGUE

IT WAS PROBABLY a good thing for Enceladian society that their Shakespearian version of post-kayfabe wrestling theater was only a flash in the pan. But it meant Overalls' run as his home world's Steve Levey was short-lived too. Soon, he found himself with no role, an outsider, a stranger in his own hometown, after all those nights dreaming of finally being home. His wife was gone. His rank at Central Command was gone. His newfound status as a hometown hero who made good had amounted to fifteen minutes of fame. He haunted his darkened house, passing, wraith-like, from room to room.

On a typical day that drifted from the last to the next like all the rest, he found his way back from a gray daydream to hear a rumbling engine. He looked outside his window and saw Maxim, the Son of Blackbird, founder and lone member of the Ring Raiders, the first MC on Enceladus, swaggering to his front door. Overalls stepped out on his front stoop. Wordlessly, they embraced. Maxim needed fellowship and Overalls needed to belong. Before long, thanks to advanced technology on Enceladus, they had fabricated a Ring Raiders cut, helmet and even a Harley for Overalls.

Steve Levey looked down from the heavens and smiled as he saw them rumble off together through the corridors of Enceladus, then he took a long puff on his cigar.

THE END

AMBUSH AT THE PALACE

A FLORIDA CRIME NOVEL, RELATED TO THE GRAPPLER CHRONICLES, COMING IN THE SPRING OF 2023: AN EXCERPT

RANDY WAS OFF SCHEDULE. He'd done the Friday Tampa to Tallahassee run many times and, being a numbers guy, he knew he was off schedule before he ever got on the road. The curtain jerker went on at eight-thirty in the old Butler Building they called the Tallahassee Sports Palace. He needed to be there just before eight o'clock when they opened up the box office (which was a cash box with spare change, a folding table and a metal chair). To get into town in time to go to the Wuv's Hamburgers he liked on North Monroe, read the *Flambeau,* enjoy a Doublefresh Burger and some Hawaiian Wuv's Juice, meant arriving no later than seven o'clock. Randy wasn't an interstate guy so he'd take 98 straight up the coast. Thunderstorms and pileups allowing, he could usually make the two hundred four mile trip in about four hours and forty-five minutes. He budgeted five. So that meant leaving Mr. Cantrell's office at the Bayfront Armory by two o'clock.

He always got on the road with a full tank. But on that hot June Friday in 1979 there was an oil crisis going on, with lines at the pump and tempers running as high as the mercury. The stop to fill up on Howard Avenue near the Armory took almost an hour and a half so instead of getting to Mr. Cantrell's office at one o'clock, he didn't arrive until after two. Randy parked around the side, came in through the front lobby, hustled down the bleachers and headed for the office. He gave a quick nod to Bobby tightening up the ring ropes and headed in.

"You're late," Cantrell said without looking up from the piles of paper an old oscillating fan moved around his desk. "I thought I paid you not to be late."

"You pay me to deliver your money, Mr. Cantrell." Randy spoke to the mostly bald back of Cantrell's head as the fan blew smoke in his face from a Salem cigarette smoldering in the ashtray on the desk.

After a few awkward moments, the old man swiveled around in his chair to face Randy. "We should have a big house up in Tallahassee. Got the Playboy up there to take on their local hero," he said. In other words, he was expecting Randy to come back with a big duffel bag full of cash after the matches in the Capital City.

"Any special instructions tonight?" Randy always asked but Mr. Cantrell seldom had any. It was more a custom, him coming by on his way to the matches around the state. Randy was on the road between six and seven days a week at least fifty weeks out of the year. His job was to secure the cash from the matches from the time the ticket taker took in the first dollar bill to the time the money was transferred to his duffel bag and brought back to the Heavyweight Championship Wrestling from Florida office of one Mr. Ernie Cantrell in Tampa. He'd had some run-ins and a couple close calls but always gotten every dime of the take back, on time, to Ernie's safe in the Bayfront Armory. He took comfort in knowing his schedule down to the minute and the mile so he could compensate for flash floods and jackknifed semis, or whatever other obstacles arose.

"Don't keep me waiting again," Cantrell said, then swiveled his chair back around, took a drag on his cigarette and started chasing little slips of paper the fan seemed always to be rearranging on his cluttered desk. Randy turned to leave but then Cantrell spun back around.

"One more thing," he said. "We got this gas shortage on so make sure you fill up."

"Already did, sir." Randy didn't bother explaining that's why he'd been late. Having served in Korea and then with the Tampa PD, he didn't come from a culture of making excuses. That helped to explain why he and Ernie Cantrell got along as well as they did.

Randy took his leave, gave a quick nod to Bobby on the way out and climbed the bleachers to the front lobby. When he got into his black '77 Cutlas Supreme the clock on the dash and his watch both read two-thirty-two. More than half an hour off schedule but he could make it up on the way and still get his Double Freshburger. Randy put the transmission in drive and pulled out onto Howard Avenue with a full tank of gas. Within a few minutes he'd gotten onto 98 North with two hundred forty-three miles to go.

At fifteen miles to the gallon with a seventeen-gallon tank, Randy could expect to make it two hundred fifty-five miles before he ran out of gas. With a two hundred forty-four mile trip that would have him coasting into Wuv's in the red but he never cut it that close. He usually stopped in Perry, about an hour out, to fill up. Then he'd stop at the twenty-four hour place in Crystal River on the way back to fill up again.

His tank was still mostly full when he passed through Spring Hill and Brooksville but he took note of the "NO GAS" notices posted over the gas price signs at local filling stations. It was a good thing he'd waited in that line on Howard Avenue before he left Tampa. Randy drove with the AC cranked and spinning the dial around to pick up local stations as he made his way up the Gulf Coast. He noticed at least one gas station in Crystal River with a tanker in the parking lot and a long line of cars out front. Must have just gotten a fuel shipment.

The stretch from Crystal River to Perry was pretty much a dead zone but once he got to Perry he was down to about a quarter tank and the "NO GAS" or "WE'RE ALL OUT" signs were up at every station. One had even put plastic garbage bags over the pump handles. He'd make it to Tallahassee but if he couldn't fill up there he'd be stuck. For the last stretch, from Perry to Wuv's in Tallahassee, Randy killed the AC to conserve fuel, rolled the windows down and popped in a Ravi Shankar eight-track, then returned to his morning meditations to allay the creeping anxiety of first being off schedule, then getting dressed down by Mr. Cantrell and now not knowing how he'd get gas to make the return run with the money from the matches at the Tallahassee Palace.

He rolled in to Wuv's at seven-nineteen that night, went in and was greeted with a smile and a copy of the *Florida Flambeau* by the manager.

"There you are," she said as she handed him the paper. "I was starting to wonder if you were coming in tonight. You're usually so punctual."

Randy just shrugged. "Thanks for holding onto the paper for me."

"Usual Doublefresh and a Hawaiian juice tonight? Any chili or fries? How 'bout a shake?"

"Just the usual," Randy said then settled up and sat down with his paper. He realized as he waited for his food that he'd done such a good job chilling himself out with his Ravi Shankar eight-track for that last stretch he hadn't even noticed if the stations he passed in Tallahassee had any gas.

Once his food arrived he set the paper aside and focused on eating quickly, then, at seven-forty-one, he headed for the matches, south on Monroe, through Frenchtown – the Black part of town – past the old and new Capitol Buildings and on through Florida State campus to Springhill Road, then out to the truck route and the optimistically named Tallahassee Sports Palace. This time he paid attention. The only station he passed without a "NO GAS" sign was already closed. He turned in to the dirt parking lot at the Palace and wove his way through the potholes and the crowd making their way up to the ticket box, then pulled around behind the building where the wrestlers parked. When he killed engine the fuel gage was all the way on E.

"Hey, Marty. Hold the door."

Marty was new in the territory. Some nights he wrestled in the openers. Tonight he wore the black and white stripes of the referee's uniform.

Randy made his way through the folding chairs and bleachers up to the front door where he could keep an eye on the ticket taker and make sure all the ones and fives and tens and twenties ended up in the metal box and not in a pocket or sock or anywhere else. He didn't announce his presence or try to hide it. The ticket takers, like dealers in a casino, knew they were being watched. They hoped only by Mr. Cantrell's bagman and not someone planning to rip them off.

About ten seconds after Randy leaned up against the wall behind the ticket taker the young guy at the table turned around and gave him a small wave. It was as if they could feel him back there. Staring at them. But Randy wasn't staring at *them*. He was counting the money coming in. At five dollars a head all he had to do was count the heads coming in the door and keep adding five each time another one did. By the time they closed up the ticket booth he usually had a pretty accurate total in his head.

Mr. Cantrell had said they were expecting a "big house" tonight. The headliner pitted "Rich" Robbie Sanborn, the "Naples Playboy" against Willie Winston, a former football player for Florida State who was a local hero but didn't get drafted to play in the NFL due to an injury. Cantrell didn't think Winston had the ringwork to make it outside of Tallahassee as a wrestler either but here they loved him and

Cantrell would back anyone who could put asses in the stands.

There were no signs that said "COLORED SECTION" in the top of the bleachers but there may as well have been. Willie Winston was Black but he was loved by the white folks in Tally too so he had all the hometown support. Robbie Sanborn was the big name heel down in southwest Florida, up to do this spot show for Cantrell in Tallahassee. Randy heard he may have timed it in conjunction with some real estate deal in Franklin County. Seems The Naples Playboy always had a few angles he was working.

Sanborn had no trouble drawing heat from the redneck and rural Black crowd in North Florida. They didn't care for Naples pretty boys with bleach blonde hair and a slightly effeminate strut. Randy had met Sanborn on a couple occasions. Always seemed like a real prick to him, in and out of the ring.

The line was steady and Randy had counted close to six thousand dollars going into the metal box so far. He looked down at his watch, eight-forty-three. The first match should have started at eight-thirty. These Friday night matches were scheduled to start later than on the weeknight cards when folks had to get up and go to work the next day. And they also always seemed to start later than advertised. Randy tried to remember which gas stations closed at what time. He didn't like the feeling of that money just piling up in the cash box and him with no reliable means to deliver it back to Tampa.

Cantrell had come up with a plan for the match where the hometown hero would keep his fans with him and the Playboy wouldn't have to take a dive for a newb like Winston. Sanborn got the crowd into it right away when he came out for his ring walk in orange trunks and blue boots, the colors of the rival Florida Gators from Gainesville. This wasn't a football game, but in Tallahassee you didn't wear orange and blue unless you were spoiling for a fight. When he paraded around the ring using his arms to mimic the gator chomp, the local cops working security started to get antsy. It was like playing with fire stoking the flames of the Seminole-Gator rivalry. The crowd shook the bleachers when Winston bounded out to the ring in Seminole garnet and gold.

With Bobby Bowden coaching, FSU had gone from a winless season in '73 to thrashing Texas Tech in the Tangerine Bowl in '77. Most importantly, they'd closed out the '78 season with a win over the Gators. And if Ernie Cantrell could cash in on a college football rivalry in the offseason to get those fans buying tickets to his wrestling matches, that's what he would do.

Sanborn let Winston look good for the first few minutes, acting like he was getting increasingly frustrated as the younger, more athletic-looking Winston got a few pops with the crowd, making the Playboy look like a cat that fell off the counter. But then, the crafty old veteran started to turn the tables on his younger foe, pulling the crowd even further into the seesaw struggle. At one point, Sanborn got Winston off balance and he seemed to twist his bad ankle – reminding the crowd of the gruesome injury he'd had back at FSU that ended his NFL prospects. After that, Sanborn looked for every opportunity to kick at, stomp on, twist or otherwise re-injure Winston's ankle. When the ref was distracted, Sanborn picked the hobbled Winston up over his head and hurled him out of the ring where he landed on the bad ankle and crumpled to the floor in agony. Marty, the referee, turned back, saw Winston outside the ring and started the ten count. The crowd screamed at the ref but he ignored them as Sanborn strutted around the ring doing the gator chomp and Winston, unable to stand after repeated attempts, was counted out. The crowd was hot, Sanborn was lucky to get out of there unscathed and Ernie Cantrell had an angle he could keep using to tell tickets.

Randy thought back through his routine and his own

performance since leaving his house that afternoon. He found little to critique in his planning. He'd thought of trying to carry spare fuel in gas cans but not in time to act on it. They weren't letting folks get more than their tanks filled at the Howard Avenue station anyway. His tactical error had been to allow rolling down the windows and listening to sitar music to distract him from paying attention to what gas stations had fuel and when they closed. He had to hope they got through the card by eleven and he could secure the take and be back on the road by eleven-fifteen. He'd have to settle up with the guy from Waverly's Furniture (their local sponsor), the concessions vendors, the souvenir table, the guy who did the ring setup, the ref and, of course, the wrestlers. Realistically, if he could be on the road by eleven-thirty he had to think he could find a gas station that was open until midnight on a Friday night in a college town. And they were probably selling more beer than gas to college students anyway, right? Randy had to hope so when he walked out to the parking lot with his brown leather duffel bag holding eight thousand two hundred twenty-four dollars of Mr. Cantrell's money and the gas gage on E.

The Cutlas sputtered a little but it turned over. He estimated he'd traveled two hundred fifty-two miles of the 255 he figured to be his maximum range. There were still rednecks hooting and hollering in the dirt parking lot, and car stereos blasting Bad Company from one side and Waylon Jennings from the other. He stowed the duffel bag on the floorboard on the passenger side with a windbreaker spread out on top of it. As Randy pulled out onto the truck route the clock on the dash read eight minutes to midnight.

As soon as he exited the ruckus of the Palace's dirt lot full of after the match partiers, the road quickly swallowed him up in a dark and quiet night, the only sound being the breeze whipping in through the open windows. There wasn't another car in sight much less a gas station when he felt the engine start to shudder. He was out of gas.

Randy eased the Cutlas over to the soft shoulder by the side of the road. He looked down instinctively to confirm the duffel bag was securely stowed in the floorboard then turned the key to the off position in the console and took it out of the ignition. He really thought he'd have had enough gas to make it to the closest station. Now he was off schedule for sure. He sat in the near dark and almost total silence. After a few minutes the hum of crickets grew in his ears and mosquitoes started finding their way in the windows. It was still hot even at midnight. As he saw it, he had three choices and he didn't like any of them.

Staying in the car with the money and doing nothing was the first option he ruled out. The second option was to put the duffel in the trunk and set out on foot. That got ruled out next. No separating himself from the money. That only left option three, take the money with him and set out on foot. He liked it only slightly more than the first two but it seemed to him the only real choice so he tossed the windbreaker onto the back seat, grabbed the duffel and a flashlight from the glovebox, then got out and started walking.

The moon provided enough light to conserve the flashlight battery. He could see well enough to notice cigarette butts, broken beer bottles and a Wuv's wrapper on the side of the road. Every once in a while a car passed. It seemed they were all going fast and either didn't see him or didn't see any reason to slow down if they did. A pickup went by coming from the direction of the matches and a few drunk hooligans in the back shouted some obscenities at him. But they didn't slow down either so he didn't worry about it. He didn't see any lights along the road. No houses. No businesses. No pay phone or filling station. Just a couple warehouses and a whole bunch of nothing.

Randy revisited his performance tally. No updates on the

planning analysis though depending on how far he ended up walking he may need to add a pair of sneakers to the crash bag in the trunk. On the performance tally, he docked himself for another unforced error for not knowing how many miles he was at this point from a hotel or truck stop or somewhere he could start the process of gaining back some of the ground he'd lost.

Weary of looking at the trail of garbage along the roadside, now including coffee grounds, diapers and a used condom, Randy allowed his line of sight to rise up into the night sky. He tried to orient himself by the stars but often found his innate understanding of numbers didn't translate as he might have liked to astronomy and sense of direction. After a few minutes of looking up into the sky with very little light pollution to mute the magnificence of the cosmos, he started to get a little dizzy, so he looked back down. As he did, he caught a glimpse of something – a shooting star, perhaps – out of the corner of his eye. When he looked back up it was gone.

It made him think about Gorpp the Grappler, who'd shown up a few years ago in Tampa and gone on to become the biggest name in professional wrestling. People asked Randy if he'd met Gorpp. He had. A couple times. Like with the Naples Playboy, the interactions were brief. Gorpp was either silent or monosyllabic. He didn't seem comfortable with or interested in conversation. It was hard to draw much in the way of conclusions from those interactions. He'd seen him wrestle and would have to say he'd never seen anyone better. And he'd seen him up close. He couldn't say if Gorpp was really from another planet, like they said, but he was one strange looking cat. No doubt about that.

Randy instead saw an orange VW Bug pull up just in front of him and idle. He slowly approached the passenger side and found the window down. He took the driver to be about his age – late 30s to early 40s – nice smile and a lowcut tube top. He held the duffel bag behind him and leaned into the window.

"You out walking after midnight, sugar?"

"I suppose," Randy said. He looked at the nothing stretching out ahead and behind him. "I appreciate you stopping."

"Where you headed?"

"Don't know for sure. Ran out of gas back there." He pointed. "Just looking for a phone or a gas station or somewhere open, I guess."

"There's not gonna be much of anything around here. If you want a lift I can take you to the filling station a few miles up ahead. I don't think they're open though."

With his head inside the car he could smell her perfume.

"I can pop the trunk for your bag there," she said, motioning to what would be the hood on most cars.

"I'll just put it down at my feet," he said. He climbed in the cramped cab and quickly found the bag wouldn't fit on the floorboard so he shoved it over their heads and into the backseat. "Sorry, did I bonk your head?"

"It's alright," she said. "Precious cargo?"

Randy gave her a half smile and reached for his seatbelt but couldn't find it. "No seatbelt?"

"Not in these old things," she said, a little too enthusiastically as she pulled back out onto the road. Once she got it up into fourth gear she offered her right hand to shake. "I'm Benny."

"Benny?"

"Yeah, 'Benny,'" she said. "As in, thanks for the ride, Benny!"

Randy offered another half-smile. "Thanks for the ride, Benny. I'm Randy, Randall."

"Well, which is it, Randy or Randall?"

"I'm just glad to meet you," he said.

She smiled back, sort of.

Before they reached the intersection they could tell the service station was closed. They pulled in to the parking lot but the payphone was busted. Randy could feel her looking at him as the car idled, headlights shining on the smashed payphone.

"I live nearby," she said. "I just ran out to get some rum so I could go sit home alone and drink and listen to Tom Waits. Big Friday night! You wanna crash on my couch, Randall?"

He looked at his watch. Way off schedule. He met her eye. He could call Mr. Cantrell from her place. "Thank you, Benny. You have a phone?"

She gave him a smirk. "Yep, I don't have much but I do have a phone."

She pulled back out onto the road and went up a little further before turning off on a dirt road into total darkness. The old VW's suspension wasn't made to bounce up and down dirt roads but something else was bothering Randy. Ever since they'd turned off the main road. He looked at Benny.

"How far down is your place?" He could hear the tremor in his voice in rhythm with the ruts in the road.

Benny kept looking straight ahead.

"Benny?"

She put her hand on Randy's leg and spoke in a deadpan only altered by the bouncing of the car on dirt and clay. "Listen to me carefully," she said. "I won't have time to repeat it." She paused. He looked at her. She kept looking straight ahead. "The guys from the pickup are waiting at the end of this road. They got cold feet when they saw you and got me to reel you in so they could ambush you. They know about the duffel bag – "

Randy whipped around to make sure it was still there.

" – They may look like drunk yahoos but they've been watching you for a while and planning this. For weeks now. Their courage may come from a bottle but there's more cunning behind this than you think. I'll slow down a little. You'll have to jump and roll. We're close enough now they can see the car and hear it. If I stop they'll know I let you go. If you jump out of the car – and leave the money – I think you might be able to get away."

"I knew you looked familiar," Randy said. "You were watching the ticket taker, weren't you?"

"No," she said. "I was watching you. I have been for a while."

Boy, the score on Randy's performance card wasn't looking good. All of a sudden it hit him. He'd allowed himself to feel superior to these hicks up here in Tallahassee and he'd underestimated them. He'd failed to pick up his surveillance and he never questioned being rescued from the side of the road in the middle of the night by a pretty and inviting lady. It was hard to think, in that moment, of anything he'd gotten right other than making sure he got his goddamn Double Freshburger and his *Flambeau* at Wuv's.

Headlights came on in front of them and the cunning hooligans jumped down from the bed of the pickup armed with bats and pipes and Lord only knew what else. Randy wrenched the steering wheel to the left and hit one of the shirtless road pirates hard enough with the car to cause a couple others to scatter. Benny hit the brakes so as not to run over the one they'd hit and as soon as they stopped another reached in and started pulling Randy out through the open window by his neck. He got a hold of his attacker's wrists and managed to twist until one snapped and both hands released their grip. Then a bat smashed through the front windshield and hit him on the shoulder with a crack and sprayed glass shards into his face. He grabbed hold of the bat and twisted it out of his assailant's hands, then turned to grab the duffel only to discover it and Benny were gone, the driver's side door left standing open.

ACKNOWLEDGMENTS

I would again like to thank my loyal first readers, Rowan and Rebecca, for their continued interest and support. Thanks as well go to Damian and Victoria for their technical support in helping to get this book over the finish line.

ABOUT THE AUTHOR

D.R. Feiler is a pen name for author Damien Filer whose works have appeared under many names, in publications ranging from *Pro Wrestling Illustrated* to the *New York Times*. He is the cofounder of an independent record label, a sought after speaker and an adjunct lecturer at a state university. He has appeared everywhere from Star Trek to the cover of a Stephen King novel. Damien has written a song with the lead singer of punk legends, the Bad Brains, and an award-winning script for a world heavyweight boxing champion. He is a graduate of Clarion Writers' Workshop at Michigan State University. He lives on planet Earth with his beautiful wife and daughter, and two silly dogs.

facebook.com/DRFeiler
twitter.com/DRFeilerAuthor
instagram.com/d.r.feiler

Made in the USA
Columbia, SC
10 November 2022

70788575R00112